'I am master here,' Suliman said under his breath, 'and here—I am the law!'

'No...I won't stay here!' Beth said heatedly.

'You are brave and spirited and I know you will fight me,' he drawled coolly. 'But it is part of our...shared fantasy, is it not, *bint*? That you will fight and I will conquer.'

Her breath caught and she said shakily, 'You will not conquer me! I want to go home right now.'

'You do not listen, *bint*,' Suliman said flatly, his mouth hardening as he looked at her. 'And you do not learn. You are my captive: I am your master. And eventually you will admit your own silent approval of this shared fantasy.'

SAHARA

DESERT DESTINY

BY

SARAH HOLLAND

MILLS & BOON LIMITED
ETON HOUSE   18-24 PARADISE ROAD
RICHMOND   SURREY   TW9 1SR

*First published in Great Britain 1991
by Mills & Boon Limited*

© Sarah Holland 1991

*Australian copyright 1991
Philippine copyright 1992
This edition 1992*

ISBN 0 263 77398 1

*Set in Times Roman 11 on 11¼ pt.
01-9201-50423 C*

Made and printed in Great Britain

CHAPTER ONE

THE sheikh towered over her, a whip in one savage hand. She knelt at his feet, sweat on her parted lips. The hot desert sun beat down on them, and as the music rent the air she inched away from him on her knees, the whip cracking mercilessly on the sand near her sprawling thighs.

The harem silks she wore were peacock-blue. Sun-kissed hair tumbled in gold curls around her ravishing face, her belly left bare and her full breasts pouting in a golden cleavage. She was covered in gold...anklets and belly-chains and bracelets of bells, and a necklace flashing at her throat.

The shiekh's whip tore the silk on her thigh and she gasped, staring up at him. He laughed and reached for her, his strong hand catching her wrist as he dragged her to her feet and inflicted a punishing kiss on her mouth.

Suddenly, the sound of hoof-beats rent the air.

'What the...?'

She was turning. They were all turning, and as they stared in shock across the golden ocean of desert they saw the sands clouding up around a pack of horses riding fast towards them.

Led by a man in white robes, the horsemen thundered nearer, and as Bethsheba stared she saw the gleam of gold on the leader's head-dress and knew he was a sheikh.

'Leave this to me!' Chris shouted from behind the cameras.

5

But Bethsheba barely heard. Her heart was thudding louder than the horses' hoofs and her eyes were riveted on the sheikh: the real sheikh, the man who rode towards her with narrowed hawk-like eyes and a mouth that could strike passion into the heart of any woman.

He was upon them now. The white stallion danced beneath him as he brought it to a halt, sand flying up as though to clothe him in the aura of a desert god.

'I am Sheikh Suliman El Khazir of the Auda Khazir!' His voice rang out in dark authority! 'And this land is mine! Who gave you permission to be here?' His English was perfect, only the slightest trace of Arabic turning his voice throaty.

'Sir——' Chris—ever the diplomat—stepped forward with a deep salaam '—my name is Chris Burton. I am in charge here. Please accept my apologies for trespassing. I had no idea I needed permission. I assumed——'

'I see clearly what you assumed, English.' The sheikh's hard mouth flickered into a cruel smile. 'But you were mistaken. This is the land of the Auda Khazir, and I am their master.'

Yes, Bethsheba thought, breathless: that dark face held the stamp of power. Deeply tanned and hard-boned, he sat astride that Arab stallion with aristocratic ease. His eyes were narrowed, hawk-like and black, and they flicked now, suddenly, in Bethsheba's direction, the look in their dark depths making her body quiver with awareness.

'Then may I again extend our apologies?' Chris Burton said with a charming smile. 'And perhaps ask your permission to continue filming here?'

The shiekh slid his dark gaze insolently over Bethsheba's body without even glancing at Chris.

'What exactly,' he asked, studying Bethsheba's full breasts and bare belly, 'are you filming?'

'A pop video,' Chris told him as Bethsheba's heartbeat thudded faster. 'We work in the music industry.'

He looked at Chris coolly. 'The girl is a singer?'

'Yes.' Chris nodded. 'A very famous singer. Her name is Bethsheba and she——'

'Sheba...?' The shiekh said under his breath, staring at her.

'Bethsheba,' Chris repeated, struggling to win over the desert leader, 'a very big star in the West. She'd sold millions of records and——'

'I care nothing for records,' said the sheikh, and nudged his white steed into motion, walking him over to Bethsheba, a look of dark intent in his eyes.

Involuntarily, Bethsheba backed in alarm.

'Don't back away from him!' Chris muttered to her.

Pulses leaping, she stood still and looked up into the face of Sheikh Suliman El Khazir. The dark eyes watched her, black and heavy lidded and intent.

'So,' he said under his breath, 'you are truly the Sheba?'

'You—you have heard of me?' she asked huskily.

'Oh, I have heard of you, *bint*!' he said softly, so softly that for a moment she wondered if he had said it at all. His mouth was curved suddenly in a smile, and she felt a shiver run through her body as though a premonition had touched her soul when he'd spoken.

Then, the sheikh turned, strong dark hands touching the leather reins as he wheeled the Arab stallion in a perfect circle and moved back with regal arrogance towards the cameras, towards the crew, towards Chris Burton.

'Very well,' he said, head lifted, 'you may continue to film on the land of Auda Khazir.'

A sigh of relief hushed through the gathered crew.

'Thank you very——' Chris began gratefully.

'But there is a price, English!' interrupted the sheikh with a slow, soft drawl, and he leant forward, one strong arm resting on the pommel of his saddle.

Chris blinked blond lashes rapidly. 'Of course!' The diplomatic mask was nailed in place as he smiled. 'Name it!'

The dark hawk-like eyes flicked suddenly to Bethsheba. 'I will hear your songbird sing.'

There was a little silence, and under his strong, arrogant gaze she felt, to her humiliation, her nipples become prominently erect beneath the blue silk harem bodice she wore. The dark eyes flicked to her face, met her gaze, and made her heart skip a beat.

'Sing?' Chris looked baffled for a moment, staring. 'You want to hear her sing? Well, sure...of course...I mean——'

'Tomorrow night!' The sheikh straightened on his horse. 'I will hear her sing at my palace. It is the House of the Seven Suns on the outskirts of Agadir, the gateway to the Western Sahara.'

'The House of the Seven Suns...' Chris was saying, mystified, and someone with initiative behind the cameras grabbed a piece of paper and wrote it down.

'It is my birthday tomorrow,' drawled the sheikh with a faint, hard smile. 'You will eat with me, Burton, while your songbird pleasures me with her voice.'

Bethsheba swallowed, her throat dry, and studied him through lashes damp with sweat as the sun burnt down on her tousled gold hair, her full cleavage and her bare arms and belly.

Chris had no choice but to make a deep salaam and say, 'We are honoured.'

The sheikh gave a thin smile, and turned his horse. 'Bring her to me tomorrow night at seven!'

Suddenly he was riding away, nudging his horse into a gallop as his men turned their horses, too, and galloped away at his side in a menacingly silent display of desert loyalty, the only sounds the thunder of hoofs.

Everything around Bethsheba felt so Western, so tame and somehow conventional. The cameras that surrounded her filled her with boredom. Just the latest in a long, long line of promotional videos for her records. Even the excitement of knowing it was a brilliant song, and would hit number one, no longer affected her.

But in the dark landscape of her mind a secret fantasy stirred in its long-forgotten, long-abandoned grave, and she knew she would have ridden away into the desert with Sheikh Suliman El Khazir had this been that dark, potent landscape instead of reality.

Suddenly she was very much looking forward to singing at his palace tomorrow night...

Next day they worked in the studio. Chris owned a villa in Tangier, and it was here that they were staying to record and film. High on a curving hill overlooking the city, the villa gave a ravishing view of flat red roofs and clean white walls leading down to the rich, spicy heart of Tangier: the bazaars and little dirty alleyways filled with jewels and rugs and spices. The wail from a nearby mosque filled the air at regular intervals and the cry of 'Allah!' echoed in the city heat.

'We'll take it once again from the top,' Chris said through Bethsheba's headphones.

'Can't you drop me in for that line?' she asked over the microphone, watching him through the smoked-glass studio windows.

'I can if you prefer not to work hard,' Chris said flatly, watching her from the control-room.

'Oh, all right, then! From the top!' And she sang the whole chorus verse again, her pride rising to the fore as always when Chris criticised her. It had always been this way between them. Their platonic relationship was like a family relationship that blended perfectly with business.

'Perfect!' Chris said when she had finished. 'Outstanding vocal! Well done, Beth!'

Bethsheba studied him, wondering why she no longer felt a thrill of pleasure when he was pleased with her. She hung her headphones on the mike, walked across the gleaming parquet floor and slid open the glass doors to the control-room.

'We'll add all the choruses tomorrow for the sampler,' Chris said.

'You don't need me for that, do you?' she asked rhetorically.

Chris replied by pressing the sampler keyboard, making Bethsheba's voice burst through the speakers, singing, 'Sheikh! Sheikh! Sh-sh-sh-sh-sheikh!'

'We'll have to release a greatest-hits album for you soon,' Prudence, her pneumatic peroxide-blonde backing singer, drawled from the sofa. 'Listen to this,' she said, flicking through last month's *Q* magazine: ' "Bethsheba's fifteenth number-one single proves the old adage that you can never underestimate the stupidity of the masses!'''

'Bastards!' said Chris.

'I never read my reviews.' Bethsheba sank on to a stool beside Chris at the control-desk and toyed idly with the sampler. 'It's too painful!'

'They're just jealous.' Chris flicked off the power and dropped a kiss on her tawny-gold head. 'It's the name of the game. Success brings criticism— failure brings praise. If you only sold ten records a month they'd call you an artist and you'd be worshipped as a cult figure.'

'Or you could always commit suicide on stage,' Prudence drawled. 'That'll get you sensational reviews!'

Chris laughed. 'Do you want to be famous or do you want to be *famous*!'

Bethsheba felt an overwhelming urge to escape again. It gnawed at her constantly these days. Her life had become a trap, and there was no way out of studio work, concerts, touring, television appearances, interviews, photograph sessions...

Suddenly the urge to escape was too strong. Her gold eyes flicked to the walls of the studio. Black walls...windowless walls...oppressive walls. No light, no view, no outside world. No sense of time; here, in this airless room with its forty-eight-track mixing-desk, it could be morning, afternoon or evening; winter, summer or spring; London, New York or Paris.

'I'm going out,' Bethsheba said suddenly, standing up.

Everyone turned to look at her. Mark, programming the drum computer, almost dropped his ice-cold beer.

'Out?' Chris frowned. 'What do you mean—out?'

'I need some air,' she said rapidly. 'I want to go out!'

'But we've got to leave in an hour.' He glanced at his watch. 'We've got to be at the sheikh's palace at Agadir at seven. It'll take at least four hours to drive there.'

'I won't be long,' she said quickly, and moved to the door.

'Wait!' Chris leapt in her way, at his most autocratic now, that RADA training leaping into evidence as his voice took on a distinctly Shakespearian ring. 'You are not, I repeat, *not* going out into town. I know you love the place, Beth, but I can't allow you to walk off into a bazaar and get lost.'

Frustration made her mouth tremble. 'But, Chris, I haven't been out of this studio since I arrived!'

'Yes, you have—you were in the desert yesterday.' He patted her head. 'Now, be a good girl and go down to the pool. Prue will go with you, won't you, Prue?'

'I'm a great chaperon,' drawled Prudence, getting to her feet.

Bethsheba struggled to be obedient, nodding and saying, 'You're right...it's best...I'll go to the pool and have a swim.' But the resentment burned in her—was Chris so blind that he didn't see how she was changing?

'Good girl.' Chris smiled and moved back to the desk. 'I'll stay here and play around with the mix. I've got a great idea for the middle section...'

They drove to Agadir in the black limousine through acres of desert on a road that seemed incongruous. It cut a black swathe through gold sands with strange rock formations on either side, scattered boulders and sand around a modern road with modern signs in blue Arabic and English.

Occasionally they passed a village of tiny bleached stone hovels without glass or windows, dogs as skinny as the boys who threw sticks at them, and old men in long caftans smoking spindly pipes.

Bethsheba sat in the back of the limousine with Prudence and Chris. They drove past Agadir as night fell. Then, suddenly, they saw the palace, standing in magnificent splendour in the centre of endless desert, its bleached and dusty walls like a Moorish castle.

'What a magnificent place!' Bethsheba was breathless with the impact of it. 'So romantic!'

'Talk about cultural differences,' Chris agreed, staring at the forbidding walls.

They swung into ancient stone gates. A vast courtyard opened out around them, fountains lilting cool water on marble, mosaic walls gleaming with palace lights under the velvet sky, guards holding guns and dogs.

'Whoever he is,' Chris murmured as the car halted, 'he's obviously very rich and very powerful. I'm glad we didn't make an enemy of him.'

Bethsheba got out of the car, trembling with nerves and excitement. Her ivory silk strapless dress clung to her slender curves. She wore a long gold silk jacket over it.

'Greetings!' A tall dark Arab in red robes appeared at the doors to welcome them. He gave a deep salaam. 'Follow me, please.'

Excitement quickened Bethsheba's step as she followed him into corridors of Moorish beauty, arched hollows in walls of blue-white mosaic, fountains in other courtyards, statues of lions and Arabic script flowing on bleached stone walls.

They swung into a final corridor. Two bare-chested Arabs in red-gold harem trousers stood guarding double doors like living art nouveau statues. The Arab leading them clapped his hands. The bare-chested Arabs swung open the double doors.

Music filled the air. Bells, tambourines, flutes and handclaps. Dazzling colours littered the magnificent Arabic ballroom, and Bethsheba stepped in, staring, her breath caught in her throat.

Bethsheba looked immediately for Sheikh Suliman El Khazir, but he was nowhere to be seen, and as her gold eyes moved restlessly around the room so she reeled under the dizzying impact of what she saw.

There were rows of richly embroidered silk cushions scattered on the floor in purple, blue, red, maroon, oxblood, royal blue, bright blue, sky-blue... Incense filled the air with a sweet, spicy opiate scent, flowing from gold filigree lamps which hung from the ceiling on gold chains. The walls were ivory stone, engraved in gold with Arabic script, and the sensual ribbons were words, words she did not understand but longed to.

'My God...' she breathed, pulses leaping at the sight of such barbaric luxury, 'I've never seen anything so beautiful!'

'I thought you were born in Bahrain?' Chris said, frowning.

'Yes,' Bethesda turned in surprise, 'but I never saw the inside of a sheikh's palace. I was only allowed to mix with army officers' children.'

'Snobbery!' Prudence's beautiful nose curled. 'Can't stand it!'

'Do you know where the word "snob" came from?' Chris asked lazily. 'It just means *sans noblesse*—without title. They used to write it next to pupils' names at Eton. Some were titled—some not. So they wrote either *noblesse* or *sans noblesse* next to your name.'

'Well, whoever this guy is,' drawled Prudence, 'he's got more *noblesse* than he knows what to do with.'

Suddenly, all music ceased. The doors at the far end of the ballroom were flung open. Footsteps approached, and as they were heard so people stood up, bowing deeply.

Sheikh Suliman El Khazir strode into the ballroom in white robes, dark eyes flashing round restlessly then fixing on Bethsheba as she met his arrogant gaze, golden head lifted, unaware of her equally regal stance.

For a second they studied each other across those bowed heads. Then a slight smile touched the hard mouth of the sheikh and he clapped his hands.

The music began again. Everyone sat down on the rich cushions. Flutes and bells and tambourines cascaded in the air as the sheikh walked towards Bethsheba.

'Good evening,' Sheikh Suliman said in that deep, rich voice as he reached them. 'Welcome to my palace.'

'Good evening,' Chris said, taking charge as usual. 'Your palace is magnificent. We are honoured to be your guests tonight.'

The sheikh inclined his head coolly, and Bethsheba noticed for the first time how very tall he was: at least four inches taller than Chris Burton, and Chris was six feet.

'Is Beth to sing in here?' Chris asked now, glancing around the room. 'She might need a microphone to be heard above——'

'She will not sing here,' said the sheikh, 'but in the Gardens of Scheherazade.' He clapped strong dark hands. 'Achmed—take Mr Burton to the gardens and allow him to inspect the stage. He may do as he wishes.'

'Thy will is my will,' said Achmed, bowing in long dark robes.

'Thank you!' Chris was more than a little taken aback. 'Right. Well—coming, Beth? Prue?'

'I... Bethsheba darted a glance at the sheikh, knowing that she preferred to stay with him, the thought of inspecting mikes and PA and running a sound-check too boring to contemplate.

'The Sheba will stay with me,' said the sheikh at once, and his strong brown fingers curled over her wrist. 'I will take care of her.'

Chris hesitated, hands thrust in black evening-trouser pockets. 'You ought to do a sound-check, Beth.'

'This way, Mr Burton,' Achmed said, 'Miss Prue...'

'You must be hungry, Sheba,' the sheikh said deeply, and his strong hand moved to the small of her back as he guided her away.

It was all very smooth, very fast, and before she knew what was happening she was walking away in gold silk beside the sheikh while Chris and Prudence were led to the Gardens of Scheherazade.

He led her down gold-scripted steps to the central floor.

'Please,' he said deeply, and gestured to the luxurious cushions scattered there, 'sit with me.'

Slowly, she sank down on them, her body as sensual and provocative as her eyes, her mouth. He smiled and sank down beside her, relaxing full-length. Their eyes met and held in a mutual acknowledgement of the strong crackle of attraction between them that was like an electric current.

He clapped his hands. A ravishing young girl in transparent scarlet harem silk appeared. Kneeling to the sheikh, she offered a long silver tray laden with delicacies. Placing it before them, she bowed, and left.

'Your slave?' Bethsheba asked with a cool glance.

'Slaves choose their own master,' he said softly, and his eyes slid to her breasts.

Her heart quickened as she felt her nipples become erect under his gaze. 'In Western civilisation, possibly. But out here in the desert?' She lifted her head. 'I think not!'

'You know the desert well?'

'I've never been to the Sahara before, but——'

'Then do not judge our ways until you understand us.' He reached out a strong hand, selected a small honey-coloured delicacy, and offered it to her. 'A crystallised bee, Sheba.'

'A bee?'

He slid it between her pink lips. 'We of course remove the sting.'

Bethsheba's mouth watered as his fingers slid the honeyed crystal inside, and the sweetness exploded on her tongue. The way he watched her, spoke to her, touched her, made her body throb with awareness, and she shifted on the silk cushions, her ivory silk dress drawing his dark gaze down over her breasts, slender waist and softly curved hips.

'You are a very beautiful woman, Sheba,' he said softly, and shifted too, reaching to touch her long gold hair. 'Hair the colour of the sun, of the sand-cat...'

She smiled. 'It's just blonde.'

'But you are blonde all over,' he said, 'are you not?'

A flush burnt her cheeks and she said acidly, 'I presume you're used to touching women whenever the mood takes you?'

'Only those who welcome my touch.'

'I'm sure you have a harem full of such women!'

'A harem!' His laughter was deep and rich as his long fingers lingered on her bare golden shoulder. 'We enter the realms of fantasy, *bint*! Western fantasy dictates that every sheikh shall have a harem quivering with nubile women ready to do his bidding!'

'And do you deny that?'

He watched her with mocking eyes. 'There are many Western fantasies of the East. Shall we explore them, Sheba?'

'I really don't mind,' she said with a light shrug, although her body was marching to the beat of his drum, and they both knew it.

'I saw a film once,' he said lightly, 'about a sheikh and a beautiful blonde Englishwoman...'

'I saw that, too,' she said, equally lightly.

'It was arousing, was it not,' the sheikh remarked lazily, 'to see him kidnap her on horseback, though she screamed and struggled? Take her to his desert camp, throw her on the pillows of his tent and...' He paused, flicking those dark eyes coolly to her enraptured face.

'She fought him!' Bethsheba said thickly, heart thumping.

'Ah, yes,' he agreed, 'she fought bravely and well. But that was part of the fantasy for them both— was it not, *bint*?'

She was quite still, unable to tear her eyes from him.

Suddenly, he was motionless too, watching her intently. 'Did you like that film, Sheba?' his dark voice asked, and she answered without thinking.

'Yes.'

CHAPTER TWO

SUDDENLY Achmed was returning at a brisk pace. Chris was behind him, and Bethsheba tensed inwardly, not wanting the intrusion of the modern world, of pop music and studios and a twentieth-century businessman. It grated harshly with this living, breathing fantasy in white robes and gold *iqal*, his hard body sprawled beside her on the silk cushions, and his dark eyes as mesmeric as his mind.

'The PA is superb!' Chris said as he reached them. 'Absolutely first class! Where on earth did you——?'

'I had them brought here this morning from Casablanca,' said the sheikh coolly.

'But this is marvellous!' Chris's handsome face was alive with pleasure. 'There's even a band, Beth! It's going to be a really good performance.'

The sheikh inclined his regal head. 'Of course.' He clapped his hands. 'Sit, please. Eat what you will. You are my guests.'

The music changed.

Out from the shadows of the pillars at the far end came dancing girls, bracelets jangling, ankle bells ringing, slender bodies twisting and turning in transparent silks of scarlet and gold, blue and gold, purple and gold. Bethsheba suddenly longed to dance with them, to wear such sensual scraps of silk, her hair flowing as she flashed out of the

shadows like a jewelled bird of paradise for her
sheikh.

Other guests arrived, and were treated with great
respect, salaams from everyone. They were obviously rich, their robes signifying authority.
Watching raptly, Bethsheba remembered Bahrain
and smiled with pleasure.

'You will sing for me very soon,' the sheikh murmured in Bethsheba's ear suddenly. 'Are you
prepared?'

'Of course,' she said with a tilt of one gold brow.
'It's my job.'

A smile touched his hard mouth. 'Then come.'
He got to his feet with arrogant grace and extended
a strong brown hand. 'I will take you to the gardens
myself.'

Together they walked across that beautiful gold-
scripted floor, he in white robes and gold *iqal*, she
in ivory silk, and, as they moved, their heads held
high, people stared at them both, but particularly
at Bethsheba, and she knew the look in their eyes.

'Your people are staring at me,' she said quietly.

'They stare because you are beautiful.'

'No,' she said frowning, 'I feel recognised. But
I'm not famous here, so——'

'So how can it be?' he agreed calmly, and clapped
his hands, signalling that the double doors leading
to the gardens should be opened. They walked
through, and the cool night air touched her cheek
as Suliman said, 'The Gardens of Scheherazade...'

The gardens were breathtaking, tiled in blue-
white mosaic, dotted with fountains and flowers and
high walls. The profusion of colour dazzled, bright
yellow marigolds mingling with the smooth pearl
of oleander, the cream clusters of jasmine, the rich
russet of harmal and henna. Slim-stemmed palms

fanned their lush silhouettes beside the draping fringes of jacaranda, and beyond blazed the most beautiful sight of all: the desert sky. So clear, so perfect—each star blazing with light and colour like a tray of diamonds on black velvet at Tiffany's.

'Do you enjoy your fame?' asked the sheikh suddenly, his deep voice startling her.

'Oh...!' She turned to find him watching her with those dark, mesmeric eyes and shrugged lightly. 'It's something I've learned to live with.'

'But do you wish it to be so, Sheba?'

She moistened her lips and found herself saying truthfully, 'I find it rather suffocating. Fame, publicity, studio work. I often feel like a caged bird.'

'A dove, *bien sûr*!' he murmured, a smile touching the hard mouth. 'And, like any dove, you long to escape.'

'Sometimes,' she admitted.

'But how,' he asked coolly, 'does a caged bird learn to be free? Perhaps it must simply find a new master.'

'I need no master,' Bethsheba said, lifting her gold head.

'Yet you describe your life as suffocating and caged,' he said calmly, and his strong hand curled at her arm. 'Are these the words of a free woman?'

She looked into his eyes and suddenly needed to change the subject. 'Have you always lived here?' she asked lightly, flicking her gaze from his to the palace walls.

The sheikh recognised why she had asked that and was faintly amused, drawling, 'No. I have another palace, deep in the heart of the Sahara. The Great Palace of Suliman.'

There was a little silence as his eyes narrowed on her, and she looked at him, suddenly realising that he expected some kind of reaction from her to those words.

'The Great Palace of Suliman?' she repeated, frowning. 'You say it as though I should have heard of it——'

'No,' he said at once, and led her to walk beside him, his hand lingering on her arm as they moved slowly, bodies in harmonious step. 'It is the palace of my ancestors. Suliman El Khazir the Great built it; he once ruled most of the Sahara. It is special to me, Sheba. And to my people.'

'I should think any palace in the middle of the Sahara would be special.'

He looked at her, then away. 'I also have a *douar*—a desert encampment—a few hours' ride from here.'

'A desert man, then?' she asked, trailing her fingers through clusters of creamy jasmine petals.

'I am.' He stopped walking and looked at her, black brows like scimitars over his dark eyes. 'I was born here, Sheba. Born to rule these people and this land. I was destined, always, to love the wild beauty of the desert; and my sense of kismet—of destiny—is stronger than any force in my life.'

She smiled. 'I understand destiny. But I don't feel I have truly found mine yet——'

'And if you did?' he asked at once, his hand tightening on her arm. 'What then, Sheba? Would you run from it? Or surrender utterly?'

'If I had a destiny,' she heard her voice say as their gazes once again locked, 'I would surrender to it utterly.'

'And feel it possess you,' he said intently.

'Yes...' Shivers ran through her, her heartbeat thudded faster, and her voice was rich with longing as she found herself saying, 'And feel it possess me.'

'Destiny often comes in the shape of another person,' he said tensely. 'If it came thus—what then? Would your surrender be...' his eyes slid suddenly to her breasts, and her heart missed a beat as she felt her nipples harden prominently under that burning gaze as though he had touched her '...as complete?' His voice roughened as his gaze flicked back to hers. 'Your possession as absolute?'

Pulse throbbing, she looked into those dark eyes and knew he was telling her something. But what? And why did she feel that somewhere, deep inside herself, she already knew?

Later, Bethsheba stood under the white heat of the spotlight on stage and sang for Sheikh Suliman El Khazir, surrounded by his guests and servants in the Gardens of Scheherazade.

Her voice floated out above the music in high, breathy seduction of her audience. The band played behind her, all Arabian and obviously experienced musicians. Prudence undulated and sang at a mike to her left. It should have been a purely professional performance—polished and skilled—but nevertheless just work.

But some divine spark had entered her, and she sang only for the sheikh, only for Suliman, her eyes closed now as she gleamed in the spotlight like a living, breathing golden statue and raised her slender arms in triumph as the song ended.

Applause burst from every corner of the gardens, and Bethsheba was elated, taking her bows with a dazzling smile, eyes flashing like yellow diamonds to Suliman for the first time since she'd begun the performance and saw him smile as he realised she had known exactly where he was sitting from the moment she'd stepped on stage.

'His Majesty Sheikh Suliman El Khazir,' Achmed said when she came off stage, 'requests that you join him at his table.'

Bethsheba swayed towards Suliman's table, her body pulsating with adrenalin, face flushed and eyes feverish, every inch a star, and revelling in it for the first time in years.

'You are a gifted songbird,' Suliman drawled as she sank on to the chair beside him, his eyes moving restlessly over her. 'Mr Burton must be very proud of his caged dove.'

Indignation made her eyes flash. 'I'm not his——' She broke off, refusing to give any more away to him than she already had tonight. With a light shrug she smiled coolly and said, 'At any rate—I'm not his *only* songbird.'

'He has many like you? Impossible! There can only be one golden-skinned Sheba!'

'I mean he has other singers. About fifteen, in fact. He runs a recording company, writes all the material, arranges, produces and—well, runs the whole show.'

'Ah.' Suliman nodded, unsmiling. 'He is your producer?'

'Yes.'

'Not your lover.'

She caught her breath, staring, silenced, her lips parted as her gaze locked into his once more and the crackle of attraction flashed between them like a tangible force.

'A simple question, *bint*,' he said softly. 'Is Burton your lover or not?'

'No!' she said under her breath, her face burning with hot colour. 'He is not my lover!' Good heavens, she had never even had a boyfriend or a stolen kiss—let alone a fully fledged lover! 'We're friends and colleagues—that's all.'

Suliman gave no reply, but his eyes darkened further, and his gaze dropped to her mouth, then away. 'How long do you intend to stay in the Sahara, *bint*?'

'Another ten days,' she said huskily, aware that her voice shook, and angry with herself for betraying the depth of her reaction to him. 'We're recording at Chris's villa in Tangier.'

'And do you have a man staying with you? A boyfriend? A——'

'No,' she said quickly, before he could mention lovers again and force that hot blush to her face.

'Family?' He was idly fingering a delicate filigree cup on the carved brass table. 'Is your family in England or here with you?'

'I have no family,' she said huskily. 'My parents died when I was fourteen.'

His lashes flickered. His gaze slid to meet hers. 'Tell me, Sheba—do you ride?'

'Ride?' The question surprised her. 'Yes—I ride very well, as a matter of fact.'

'Good. Then tomorrow you will ride with me.'

'Tomorrow!' Her eyes widened. 'I don't know if——'

'Here,' he said coolly, 'I am but a few hours' drive from Tangier. I have a stable of pure-bred horses, and the Sahara surrounds me. Why should you not come here to ride with me?'

'Well, I don't know if Chris would altogether approve and——'

'We shall not tell him,' drawled the sheikh, a smile touching his hard mouth. 'It will be our secret.

Our secret...' his gaze slid to her breasts, then up to her eyes again '...fantasy. Hmm?'

Bethsheba's mouth went dry. She felt suddenly unable to reply, her heart drumming wildly.

'You will be my golden-haired Englishwoman,' Suliman said under his breath, 'and I your sheikh. Together we will live out our fantasy and surrender ourselves to destiny.'

She was staring at him through gold lashes, her lips parted, face flushed, eyes glittering, and as she remained silent so her breasts rose and fell unsteadily with the thud of her heart.

'Say yes, Sheba,' Suliman's eyes never wavered, 'and it shall be done.'

Bethsheba's voice whispered, 'Yes...'

She woke next morning to the sound of 'Haya alla Salat!' echoing across the city of Tangier from the mosque tower. Suliman's face leapt into her mind and she sat up in bed with a gasp, a hand clutching her heart as the pace leapt.

Had she really agreed to ride with him at three this afternoon? She must have been out of her mind! Of course she couldn't ride with him, or even consider going back to his palace!

Bethsheba spent the morning working in the studio. They were laying down the backing vocals on various tracks, and it was harder work than the lead vocal because it was a rather bitty job and intensely repetitive. Chris cheered them up by doing the 'To be or not to be' monologue from *Hamlet* every time they wound the tape back. But Bethsheba had heard him do it a million times before, and it had begun to grate on her nerves.

Bethsheba felt guilty as she watched Chris through the glass panel. She owed him everything—how could she be so mean as to feel bored with the friend who had saved her from penury?

Christopher Burton had discovered Bethsheba when she was fifteen and singing with an unknown band in a dingy London pub. Obviously under age, she had been desperate for money and for something to cling to that was hers.

Her parents had been killed in a car crash when she was fourteen. She had been living with her maiden aunt for a year, and felt restless, trapped, alone and unhappy. With few friends and no money, Bethsheba had been desperate for someone to come along and help her.

Chris recognised her talent as well as her desperation, and took her under his wing.

At that time, Chris had a small twenty-four-track studio in a London suburb. Working every hour of the day, he too was desperate: desperate to finally succeed in the music business.

Bethsheba learnt the ropes of the industry with him, watching him write, record, arrange and produce song after song, then suffer the painful setbacks and frustrations of life on the fringes of the music business.

She virtually lived in that studio for three years. They rarely performed live in the end; just spent endless hours recording, followed by more endless hours hiking their demos around major record labels, trying for a deal.

Eventually Chris lost his temper with the major labels. In a whirlwind of furious determination he formed his own record company, released his own singles, and pushed Bethsheba as his first release.

He had to mortgage his house to do it. Everything was riding on Bethsheba's single, and she suffered agonies of guilt as they waited for DJs to play it, magazines to talk about it, and the public to buy it.

The record went to number one and stayed there for eight weeks.

Over the next four years Bethsheba released fifteen records, all of which went to number one. Teen magazines featured her continually, television videos made hit after hit.

Now Chris Burton was the biggest force in the music industry. Everyone wanted to work with him. He had a stable of international stars and more money than he could even count.

But Bethsheba was still his biggest star—and his favourite, for she had been there with him at the beginning, in the dark ages, when they had lived on black tea, chips and grim determination.

'Let's have lunch out!' Chris said when they had finally finished recording. 'Go to the kasbah, get some knick-knacks, discover an intriguing harem, perhaps.'

'I'm rather tired,' Bethsheba heard herself say. 'I think I'll stay home and get some rest.' As the words left her mouth her stomach started to churn and she knew she was going to Suliman's palace.

They left on foot, and Bethsheba watched them go, her body alive with sick excitement. As soon as they had disappeared from view in their bright summer clothes, she raced upstairs, tugged on cream jodhpurs, a white shirt, long black boots and brushed her tousled curls into a mass of silk, then added a dash of pink gloss to her mouth for luck and rang down to the kitchen to get the car keys.

'Got bored and decided to go sightseeing in Rabat,' she wrote on a piece of paper. 'Might have dinner there. Don't worry.'

Leaving the note on the kitchen table, she slipped out of the front door so that Mohammed, their manservant, would not see her leaving and ask awkward questions about her riding outfit.

The drive to the sheikh's palace was long but relatively easy, a straight road, more or less, all the way there. As she approached the palace from Agadir she began to panic again, her stomach churning and her mouth as dry as ashes.

But as she drove through the main gates, and saw Achmed waiting for her at the doors, her stomach lurched with excitement. Suliman had not forgotten either.

The courtyard was so different by daylight—there were stone arcades and guards with dogs and a slumbrous air of mystery about it; fountains gushing into sculpted marble, greenery hanging from meshed wood balconies, and the dogs were roused from their slumber, barking as Bethsheba stepped from the car.

'Greetings, *sitt*.' Achmed gave a deep salaam. 'The sheikh is expecting you. Please to follow me.'

Locking the car door, she shoved her keys in her handbag and followed Achmed into the palace. This time she was led a different way. The cool arcades with high Moorish arches were carved with Arabesque script, and small alcoves with richly embroidered divans nestled along the way, the scent of spicy coffee clinging to the air and the low murmur of Arabic voices lazy in the hot afternoon. Obviously, these were the day quarters.

Achmed stopped outside a purple hanging, swept it aside and gestured for her to enter.

The room was vibrant with colour and brassware. Incense filled the air, cushions littered the floor, and everywhere was the stamp of barbaric luxury that seduced her with its blatant sensuality.

'So, Sheba.' Suliman stood at the far end of the room, magnificent in white robes and gold *iqal*, oxblood riding boots on his strong legs, the dark blue and red of his shirt deepening that skin to mahogany. 'You have kept our appointment.'

Her heart missed several beats. 'I always keep my promises.'

The hard mouth curled. 'So do I, *bint*!' he said softly, and the look in those dark eyes made her body throb in response to him as he stepped forward, tall, primitive and magnificent. 'Come.' He took her hand. 'Let us ride while the sun lights our way!' He led her across the room and into the corridor, drawling, 'We start as we mean to go on—the hawk leading the dove!'

Bethsheba laughed, allowing him to lead her along the cool arcade. 'The hawk and the dove...! Arabia...!'

'You embrace my culture,' Suliman observed, flicking a glance at her. 'I have noticed it before.'

'I find it very beautiful,' she agreed.

'And it is,' he drawled coolly, 'particularly in regard to women. Here, our women are admired for everything that is uniquely feminine about them. They are the goddesses of our desires, our hearts, our childhood—and we anoint them with our love.'

'That is not the Western view of the East,' she said.

'You are but one woman,' he pointed out, 'not one quarter of the world, and it is your view of my culture that I desire, not theirs.'

Suddenly they reached a vast arched doorway, and beyond it lay the bleached stone-dust of a courtyard. The scent of horses, of manure, of leather and of sweat pervaded the air.

A groom in grubby beige jellaba led two horses to them. A white Arab stallion and a gold Arab stallion with a mane the colour of honey. Bethsheba was handed a riding whip, and the groom made a bridge with his hands for her to mount the gold-coloured horse.

She mounted, laughing with a sudden rush of excitement as she sat astride that honey-coloured stallion and felt it dance beneath her as the sheikh swung on to his powerful white steed and met her gaze, laughing also.

'You are keen, *bint*!' he shouted across to her, and kicked his horse. 'Let us ride!'

They cantered out of the courtyard, hoofs clattering as the men cried in Arabic, hands raised in salute to their sheikh as he thundered into the desert, white robes flowing.

Exhilarated, the wind in her hair and sand stinging her face, Bethsheba galloped beside her sheikh and saw the light of dreams in the blue, blue sky above that ocean of golden sand. She felt brave and beautiful and free, the scent of horseflesh in her nostrils and the feeling of power as she rode fast, fast, faster.

The spurs on the heels of Suliman's dark red boots flashed gold in the hot sun. His head-dress flashed back to show the strength of his jaw, the narrowed determination of his dark eyes.

Desert landscape engulfed them, a great silence broken only by the sound of their horses' hoofs. She saw thick clumps of greenery strangled by clustered boulders near a well, and the dusty white gleam of dead animals' bones close by. Sweat covered her face and body, the saddle thudded against her thighs, her hair whipped back in a golden, tousled banner.

How far had they come? The sun was a furnace in the sky. There was nothing, had been nothing, for miles, and still they rode, still they bore down across the desert as a hawk flew overhead with a piercing cry.

'Stop!' Bethsheba reined in her horse suddenly, but Suliman rode on, and she was left cantering in a wide circle, struggling to prevent her horse following its master. 'Stop!'

Suliman reined in his horse, a quick look over one shoulder making his eyes narrow as he turned, cantering back to her, his dark, handsome face sheened with sweat.

'What is it?' he called harshly. 'Do you need water?'

'Why didn't you stop earlier?' she demanded angrily. 'You heard me calling!'

'We have only two hours before sunset,' he said, black brows meeting like scimitars above his arrogant eyes. 'We must reach the *douar* before dark.'

Her breath caught. 'The *douar*!' She knew what that meant! It conjured up a world of long ago, a world she had almost forgotten: of tents and gold sands and elegant men and women drinking hot mint tea at trestle-tables in the sun.

'Come!' Suliman waited, stallion dancing beneath his powerful thighs. 'Let us waste no more time!'

'I can't go there with you!' Bethsheba cried hoarsely. 'Not there!'

'But you must!' The dark eyes flashed. 'It is written.'

'It is not written!' she cried fiercely. 'It is not written and I won't go there with you!' Turning her horse, she tried to kick it back the way they had come, but it whinnied, worried and unsettled.

'You cannot go back!' Suliman shouted. 'Not without me!'

'I can and I will!' Fear made her whip the horse sharply on its flanks as it danced out of control.

The horse rose up in angry protest, and Bethsheba cried out in shock as she was flung backwards into the air. The last thing she saw was a blur of white Arab robes and white horse thundered towards her as the sand slammed into her and blackness claimed her.

CHAPTER THREE

THE jingle of the harness soothed Bethsheba, the swaying motion of the Sheikh's horse lulling her continually back into sleep. Occasionally, she opened her eyes, felt the stabs of agony in her head, and slipped back into unconsciousness, unable or unwilling to face what was happening.

The sheikh's chest was strong and warm and comforting. Her face rested against it, her nostrils breathing in the scent of his flesh, and sometimes when her lids flickered open she looked drowsily at that tanned skin and the dark hairs that grew on it and thought of Arabia as though it were a dream; a colourful vivid dream of gold and silk and all the perfumes. The air grew steadily cooler. The sands, once gold, were now cool pink as the sun began to set, and the next time her eyes flickered open she saw the desert was lilac, then purple, then, finally, black.

Suddenly she heard voices and the crackle of wood fires, and when the horse came to a standstill she knew they had reached the *douar*.

'Awake, Sheba.' Suliman's deep voice echoed in his chest. 'Awake and behold your dream.'

Opening her eyes, she looked up into his hard, handsome face, and for a moment saw only his features; the heavy-lidded eyes, the strong arrogant nose and the firm sensual mouth below.

Then she saw beyond and knew it was night. Camp-fires flickered and spat in the darkness. Hair tents were dotted around the encampment, horses tethered beneath a tree, and the cool waters of the oasis gleamed with starlight from above. Men and the shadows of men were all about. They wore turbans and jellabas, some carried guns, some stood guard and some sat by the fires, eating.

'Is it to your taste, Sheba?' Suliman asked with a hard smile. 'The *douar* of your fantasies?'

'No!' The fierce cry was weak, but her eyes flashed gold fire. 'You must take me back at once.'

He laughed, and suddenly dismounted, catching Bethsheba before she unbalanced. His strong arms were around her, holding her as he strode in dark red boots and white robes towards the royal tent.

A servant leapt to sweep the tent flap aside. Suliman carried Bethsheba in as though she were a gazelle, and her startled eyes took in the luxurious surroundings; the royal blue cloth walls of the tent, the embroidered rugs, low brass trestle-table covered in Arabesque script, and the central bed of silk cushions.

The sheikh laid her on the bed of cushions. 'How is your head, Sheba?' he asked, sprawling beside her, his dark face above hers as he studied her. 'You fell on the slope of a dune and your fall was softened. But still you lost consciousness...'

'It throbs a little,' she admitted, gold eyes wary. 'But you must take me back, Suliman! You cannot keep me——'

'You are my prisoner now, *bint*!' he said softly, and his dark eyes mocked her as he flicked a cool, proprietorial gaze to her mouth. 'And you will do my bidding!'

'You're out of your mind,' she whispered, but her head was thudding like a drum and she could not take her eyes off that firm, sensual mouth. 'You

must know that what you've done is against the
law.'

'I am master here,' he said under his breath, 'and
here—I am the law!'

'No...!' Her heart stopped and she tried to sit
up.

'Lie back, *bint*!' he said, pushing her down again
into the cushions. 'And accept your fate!'

'I will not!' she said heatedly, 'I won't stay here
a——' The tent flap was swept aside, silencing her
protest.

A servant entered in white jellaba and turban.
He carried an ornate carved brass tray. On it, a
coffee-pot gleamed, two brass filigree cups and a
brass plate holding squares of halva, Turkish delight and spicy biscuits. He bowed low, placed the
tray on a side-table, and said something respectful
to his master.

'What did he say?' Bethsheba asked as the
servant left. 'That he disapproves of your kid-
napping an English girl?'

The sheikh laughed under his breath. 'He would
not dare, *bint*!'

'And I suppose you think I shouldn't dare either.'
Rebellion flashed in her eyes.

'You are brave and spirited, and I know you will
fight me,' he drawled coolly, one strong hand firm
on her hip as he held her captive, 'but it is part of
our...shared fantasy, is it not, *bint*? That you will
fight and I will conquer?'

Her breath caught and she said shakily, 'You will
not conquer me!'

Suliman smiled slowly and flicked his gaze from
her to the table beside them. 'Come. You need to
rest and eat. Have some coffee and sweetmeats.

They are prepared specially for you by one of my handmaidens in the——'

'I don't want any sweetmeats!' she said, heart thumping at the nearness of his hard body and the sexual threat implicit in that soft, dark voice. 'I want to go home right now!'

'You do not listen, *bint*,' Suliman said flatly, mouth hardening as he looked back at her. 'And you do not learn. You are my captive: I am your master. And eventually, *bint*, you will admit your own silent approval of this shared fantasy.'

She stared, breathless, heart thudding. 'My approval! What do you mean—my approval?'

'We discussed it in great detail last night,' he said softly, and the long fingers selected a sweetmeat for her, sliding it on to her lips and watching her with a slow, lazy smile.

'We did not!' She pushed the sweetmeat away from her mouth with a shaking hand.

'I made myself more than clear,' the sheikh told her, and allowed his gaze to move insolently, possessively over her body, resting on the full breasts beneath her white blouse. 'And you, Sheba, responded in kind.'

'No...' She knew his gaze was provoking her to remember the way her breasts had swollen under his gaze then, as they did now, and the erection of her pink nipples only served to humiliate her further as she felt the excitement shiver through her.

'Yes.' His strong hand moved slowly to the buttons on her blouse and slid one open while she stared, trembling, hypnotised by those eyes. 'You welcome your destiny, and your ultimate surrender.'

'I don't!' she protested, then gasped, face flushing scarlet with hot arousal as Suliman's strong

fingers slid over her breast and they both felt her
taut nipples burn in electric response to his touch.

'Your body betrays you,' he said softly, and as
his head lowered to block out the light Bethsheba
heard herself give a faint moan, eyes closing helplessly as that hard mouth took possession of hers.

She struggled, but he pinned her arms to the splay
of cushions. She cried out but he silenced her with
his mouth, and as she lay helpless beneath him the
blood raced through her body with a wild throb of
excitement that made her moan as his kiss took fire,
pulling her down into a sudden dark flare of hot
desire that made her gasp against his mouth.

'So.' Suliman raised his dark head, breathing
roughly, his face flushed as he watched her, and the
soft sound of desert sands blowing in the night air
came from outside the tent. 'Let us have no more
protests or denials, *bint*!'

He got to his feet and reached for the brass
coffee-pot, pouring hot spicy coffee into the two
cups.

Bethsheba watched him, intolerably aroused, intolerably confused, and unbelievably angry with
him for kissing her like that. How dared he? How
dared he bring her here against her will, kidnap her
and put her in his desert encampment specifically
to play some vile game with her that would end in
her complete physical surrender to him...?

She hated him! Her eyes moved over his strong
back, his arrogant head, and she said hoarsely, 'You
think you can get away with this, but you're wrong!
Chris will be frantic when I don't come back! He'll
look for me, and——'

'And where will he look?' Suliman drawled
coolly, turning, and handing her a cup of rich spicy
coffee. 'At my palace of Agadir? What will he find

there? Nothing but an abandoned car and my men ready with explanations.'

'The car will be proof enough,' she said fiercely, sitting up. 'He'll inform the authorities at once and——'

'And the authorities will read the note attached to the car.' Suliman watched her, mockery in his eyes, his stance arrogant as he raised the brass filigree cup to his lips and drank.

'What note?' she demanded, her heart missing a beat.

'The note I had drafted before you arrived, *chérie*. The note telling Burton that you requested a tour of my land, many days' ride, in order to give your work new depth.'

She stared, breathless, horrified, then said on a rush, 'You don't seriously expect me to believe that?'

'Why not?' he drawled. 'In America I believe it is called method acting.'

Her mouth tightened. 'Chris went to RADA and has often discussed acting with me. He knows I'm not an actress—and certainly not interested in the Stanislavsky method!'

'Yet you were acting in the desert not three days ago.'

'For a pop video! It's hardly the same thing!'

'But it will give me the time I need, *bint*,' he said softly, 'and that, I assure you, is all I require from your friend Burton!'

Fear shot through her and she said hoarsely, 'Chris has known me for years. He'll know something's wrong. He knows me better than anyone in my life. He's almost family to me, and I to him!'

'No one can ever be sure of the contents of another's heart and mind,' Suliman said coolly, draining his coffee and setting the cup back on the brass tray.

'You say that,' Bethsheba's eyes were angry and frightened, 'yet you insist you saw silent approval in my eyes last night!'

He laughed softly. 'I saw more than silent approval when I kissed you just now, *bint*!'

Hot colour stung her cheeks and rage made her tremble as she stared at him, unable to reply for fear she would scream at him like a banshee and fly at him, hitting him for speaking such a humiliating truth.

Suliman laughed again, and turned, walking to the tent flap, saying, 'I will send a girl to you with water and fresh clothing. When it is time to eat you will be sent for.'

Fury overwhelmed her. Her shaking hands closed over a silk cushion and she found herself hurling it at his arrogant head as he swept the tent flap aside. 'Go to hell, you arrogant bastard!' she shouted hoarsely, but the cushion hit the side of the tent with a dull thud, and the sheikh's mocking laughter echoed in her ears to increase her rage and sense of helplessness.

In the dusky corners of the tent, cassia oil burnt in lamps that hung from tent-poles, and the rich drapes of royal blue seemed to mock her, saying, 'I am master here and you shall do my bidding.'

The hell I will! she thought furiously, almost gnashing her teeth; then she realised that her hands still shook, and she struggled for self-control, for the dignity that was left her. Closing her eyes, she drew long, deep breaths, momentary calm flooding her.

Suliman believed she had given her consent to this barbaric fantasy, and, even though her pride rose up in furious denial, she knew deep inside that the excitement had flashed from her eyes and communicated itself to him. However much she hated herself for having got herself in this position, she knew she had been at fault—partially.

But she hadn't meant this to happen! Panic flooded her, and she reached for her coffee with trembling hands, drinking deep, suddenly realising that she was struck by a raging thirst. She poured another cup and drank deep of the spicy coffee, and her hands reached for sweet, sticky halva and Turkish delight and biscuits as she remembered she had not eaten since this morning's meagre breakfast of fruit.

The tent flap was swept aside. Bethsheba's eyes flashed to the entrance, and stared at the shadowy figure there.

'I am Khalisha.' The girl was ravishing, her voice as beautifully Arabian as her face. 'My lord sent me to wash and clothe you.'

'How kind of him,' Bethsheba said through tight lips.

'Is the *sitt* ready?' Khalisha moved into the dim gold light of the tent, and Bethsheba stared in admiration. She was as slender as a gazelle, dusky-skinned, with long black hair and deep, lustrous eyes of brown above high cheekbones and a small dark red mouth. The purple silk of her harem trousers was edged with gold, as was her bodice, and little purple slippers on her feet were embroidered with gold.

''I'm sorry, Khalisha,' Bethsheba said angrily, unable to swallow her rage, 'I don't wish to offend you—but nor do I wish to be washed and clothed like a sacrifice for your master!'

'A sacrifice?' The girl's dark brows met over her lustrous eyes in a frown.

'I was brought here against my will and——'

'I know nothing of this,' said Khalisha at once, cool and serene as she moved further into the tent. 'I know only the orders that my lord gave me.'

'Your lord!' Her nose wrinkled the pent-up anger. 'He's not your lord, he's just——'

'He is my lord, *sitt*. And without him my people would be scattered in the desert as the wind scatters dead men's bones.' Pride of her race and heritage made the girl even more beautiful.

Getting to her feet, Bethsheba said, 'Is there a bathroom I am to use?'

'No. The *sitt* may wash behind the shiraz.'

Bethsheba looked at once to the back of the tent where a selection of gorgeously patterned shiraz rugs hung from poles to form a protective covering where she might bathe. Memories of Bahrain flooded through her at the sight of the rugs, and she moved slowly towards them.

Khalisha held one up to let her pass, and gold bangles jangled softly on her dusky-skinned arm as she watched Bethsheba. Behind the rugs was a little makeshift room, with a bowl, soaps, scents, a dark blue towel and a small mirror.

Khalisha emptied her own jug of water into the bowl. Steam rose from it, scented steam, which made the room feel even more Eastern. Khalisha turned to Bethsheba to unbutton her blouse.

'I can do that!' Bethsheba jumped back from the girl's fingers, shocked.

'The *sitt* will find it more pleasant if she is bathed by another.'

Flushing, Bethsheba said, 'It is not my way, Khalisha! In England, we bathe alone!'

'I have heard it is so.' Khalisha nodded. 'But I am glad to be of a more hot-blooded and sensual race. Here, we are taught to give our bodies the pleasure they crave.'

'We consider ourselves to be a sensual race,' she said defensively.

'Yet you bathe alone?' Khalisha smiled, eyes gently mocking. 'Come! The *sitt* is weary and I am fresh. Close your eyes and let me wash the scent of the horse and the desert from your body!'

Feeling she now had something to prove, Bethsheba allowed Khalisha to undress her. The white blouse fell to the floor, followed by her lacy white bra, and she kept her eyes closed, burning with embarrassment, but refusing to show it. No doubt they would gossip about the cold-blooded English girl around the camp-fires tonight if she refused to let Khalisha wash her! Yet, after the girl had tugged Bethsheba's jodhpurs off, she couldn't help feeling a leap of shame as her lace panties followed them a moment later and she stood naked at last.

There was a splash of scented water, then Khalisha's hand guiding a soft sponge over Bethsheba's slim thighs. Gradually, she began to relax. The warm water slid softly over her aching shoulders, her back, and her joints began to unbend until at last her eyes flickered open and her shame receded in the trappings of the sensual Orient all around her.

'Truly,' Khalisha said suddenly, 'the *sitt* is as beautiful as I had heard.'

'You had heard?' Bethsheba stared down at the girl who knelt at her feet.

'It was whispered this morning that you would arrive. They said my lord the sheikh had found his

Sheba, and that she was as beautiful as it was written she would be.'

Bethsheba stared, incredulous. 'Written!'

'Now that I see you,' said Khalisha, 'I see they did not lie. The *sitt* is the Sheba with hair of gold and skin the colour of the sand-cat. Truly, you are the she-cat.'

'The she-cat?' Bethsheba was frowning, completely bewildered and suddenly even more uneasy about her situation. 'But what does that mean? And why do you call me Sheba, as Sheikh Suliman does?'

'It is written,' Khalisha said simply, and picked up the royal blue towel to dry her body.

'Can't you tell me what is written?' Bethsheba studied her. 'I must know what you——'

'I have said enough.' Khalisha's mouth tightened.

Bethsheba sighed, then changed tack, asking, 'Where are we?'

'In the Sahara.'

'Yes,' she smiled, 'but where exactly in the Sahara?'

'I will not help you saddle a horse and escape, *sitt*.'

'Khalisha, can't you see how I feel?' Bethsheba said at once. 'I'm a prisoner here!'

Suddenly Khalisha got to her feet, small mouth tightening as she said, 'I know nothing of this, and my lord will be angry with me if I say more. Come! Stand, please. I will dress you and go.'

Bewildered, she got to her feet, staring at the girl, who bent to get her clothes. Bethsheba's body was partially reflected in the mirror; she looked leonine, gold and scented and beautiful.

'You will wear these.' Khalisha presented her with a luxurious pile of gold silk clothes, jewellery, slippers and make-up of kohl, henna and red-staining cream in small earthenware pots.

Bethsheba's mouth tightened, but she obediently slipped into the gold silk briefs, the tiny scrap so fragile, so luxurious that she felt almost nude in them. She searched for a bra and found only a gold silk caftan remained.

'Am I not to wear a bra?'

Khalisha shook her head. 'My lord does not wish it.'

Bethsheba's eyes flared angrily. 'Your lord is a selfish, arrogant——'

'He is a prince of royal blood, *sitt*!' Khalisha's eyes flared back, just as angry suddenly. 'And you are honoured to be chosen by one such as him!'

Shocked by the girl's outburst, Bethsheba realised now that she was jealous. Jealousy! she thought, staring as Khalisha flushed betrayingly and bent her head, mouth angry.

'Khalisha...' Bethsheba reached out to comfort her '...I'm sorry if I trod on your feelings. But you must understand—I've been brought here against my will, and I don't want to stay. Certainly not to be "chosen" by an arrogant sheikh to——'

'The sheikh is arrogant, yes!' Khalisha's head lifted angriiy. 'But he is magnificent in his arrogance! He would make a woman cry with pleasure if she was lucky enough to be chosen to lie in his arms! Yet all you can do, English *sitt*, is to——'

'Enough!' Sheikh Suliman El Khazir's voice cracked like a whip from the main entrance to the tent, making Bethsheba jump out of her skin, her heart suddenly banging like a drum.

Khalisha gasped and turned. The sheikh's approaching footsteps were accompanied by bitten-

out words in Arabic, and then the shiraz rug was
swept angrily aside.

'No!' Bethsheba cried instinctively, whirling to
stare at his hard face, her hands up to protect herself
from his searing gaze as he stopped dead, staring
down at her almost nude body clothed only in
transparent gold silk briefs.

There was an electric silence. She couldn't look
him in the face, her mouth open with shock, her
hands shaking as she realised there was nowhere to
hide herself from his burningly intense gaze.

Khalisha threw herself at his feet. He stood
watching her, unmoved, and when she whispered
her apologies to his dark leather boots he said
something harsh in Arabic and lifted her to her feet
with a strong hand. She gave a muffled sob, bowed
to him, then ran from the tent, ankle bracelets jin-
gling with tiny gold bells as she moved.

'Please!' Bethsheba said hoarsely as the sheikh
continued to stand directly in front of her, eyes fixed
intently on her body. 'Get out! Leave me to dress!'

He watched her in an electrifying silence,
breathing thickly. Then his nostrils flared, his hands
shot out, and he dragged her arms from her breasts
as she cried out and struggled, laying her bare to
his piercing gaze.

'Don't...' she whispered thickly, heart banging
as she squirmed desperately to hide her nudity from
him. 'Please...'

He breathed harshly, every muscle taut as he
stared at her erect nipples. Then he was dragging
her towards him, his dark head swooping, and as
that hard hot mouth fastened on her breast she gave
a low shuddering cry of fierce pleasure, her head
flung back as her legs turned to molten lava and
desire flashed between them like a forest fire.

Suddenly she was released. She swayed, dazed, flushed and fevered, almost stumbling aside in a tide of shaking passion. The sheikh stood a few inches from her, his back to her, and to her intense fury she felt sharp disappointment flood her. She fought that disappointment, hating herself bitterly for wanting him to go further.

'You can't do this,' she heard her voice say in hoarse protest as she snatched up the gold silk caftan and held it protectively against herself. 'You can't keep me here as though I had no life of my own, no will of my own and no rights of my own!'

'You will stay,' he said thickly without turning, and he breathed harshly as though the fierce desire flooded him with as much violence as it did her. 'It is my will!'

'At least tell me why!' she demanded fiercely. 'At least tell me that!'

'It is written,' he said under his breath, and the light of the cassia-oil lamps flickered softly as a desert breeze ruffled the sides of the tent.

'I'm sick to death of hearing that phrase as though I didn't exist and the only important thing was something written somewhere I don't even know about!'

He turned, dark eyes formidable. 'You will stay, Sheba!' he said tightly. 'It is my will!'

Her mouth trembled as she met that commanding gaze. 'Chris will come for me! He's not going to believe that phoney note for a second! He'll know perfectly well that something's wrong, and he'll move heaven and earth to find me!'

'And when he does he will fight me for the right to possess you,' Suliman bit out. 'For now I have you, Sheba, I will not let you go!' His lips curled with angry disdain. 'Certainly not to your English master!'

'He's not my master!' she denied furiously, indignation burning in her voice.

'Is he not, *bint*?' Suliman said tightly. 'Does he not tell you when to work and when to sleep? Does he not pick out your clothes and send you to bathe? Does he not run your life and——'

'He's my producer!'

'He is your master,' he bit out.

There was a tense silence. She stared at him, fury in her eyes and in every line of her body as she held the caftan up to cover her nudity and her eyes warred with his.

'But now I am your master,' Suliman said under his breath, eyes flicking over her with possessive determination. 'And you will do my bidding!'

'I'd rather die!' she said fiercely, her voice shaking, struggling to deny the shivers of arousal at his words, at his look, at his remembered touch. 'I'd rather die than do anything you asked of me!'

He laughed softly, and mockery entered the dark eyes. 'A shame, *bint*. For, if you do not appear at my supper-table within the half-hour, I will come to you and make you recognise your new master as I take possession of that...' his eyes flashed slowly, insolently, possessively over her trembling body '...which is mine!'

CHAPTER FOUR

THE SHEIKH strode from the tent, and Bethsheba stood trembling as she watched the tent flap fall back into place behind him. The seriousness of her position here was beginning to sink in. She sank weakly to the floor of the tent and leant against the shiraz rugs behind her.

There was only one way to end this disaster: she must escape.

With renewed confidence, she stood up and began to dress. The gold silk caftan flowed over her body. The soft gold slippers fitted her perfectly. She fastened the gold-belled bracelets on her ankles, threaded the gold-meshed earrings in her lobes, and slid the gold chain around her neck.

She moved to the mirror, sank, crosslegged, before it, and picked up the make-up pots Khalisha had brought. She enjoyed them, lining her eyes with black kohl, staining her lips red, darkening her eyelids with henna.

When she was ready she went outside.

Flickering camp-fires lit the darkness. Robed figures moved in the gold firelight. The scent of rich food assailed her nostrils and she realised she was starving.

Suliman was waiting for her, framed against the firelight. He had washed and changed too. The dark blue caftan he wore made him look deeply attractive, the tanned throat and dark chest-hairs clearly visible where the caftan parted in a deep V.

His bare feet were thrust into gold sandals, and Bethsheba knew instinctively that he was naked beneath that caftan; knew it, and felt her body leap with arousal.

'You are more beautiful than Scheherazade,' Suliman said deeply, and extended a strong brown hand. 'Come. Dine with me.'

His people fell silent, watching them walk to the table and sit down.

'They're staring again,' Bethsheba said under her breath as she sank on to the chair beside Suliman. Then she asked suddenly, 'Who is the Sheba, Suliman? The one you speak of when——'

'It is not the time, *bint*, to reveal all secrets to you.' His strong hand closed over hers, making her pulses leap. 'Accept those I have already bestowed on you and be patient.'

'What secrets have you bestowed?'

'The secrets of my desires,' he said, a smile on his hard mouth.

'You want to rape me!' she said angrily. 'You've made yourself more than clear on that score!'

'If I wanted to rape you, *bint*, you would now be sprawled naked across the cushions of my tent!'

'Oh...!' Her heart stopped beating.

'But,' Suliman said deeply, turning her wrist and lifting it to press his hard mouth against it, 'as you can see, I am not so barbaric as to destroy your innocence with brutal indifference to your dignity!'

'But you do want me. And you will force me if I refuse!'

'You will not refuse, and there will be no force.' His strong fingers slid to the pulse that throbbed at her wrist. 'Your heart flutters like the wings of a captive bird just at my touch. Can you deny you tremble not only with fear but with excitement too?'

'I deny it absolutely!' she said breathlessly.

'Then you deny yourself!' he said deeply, 'and also deny the growing demands of your womanhood.'

'That's not true!' Her face ran with angry colour. 'I'm refusing to be treated as the plaything of a bored sheikh!'

'Yet fantasy is the plaything of both men and women, is it not?' he asked coolly. 'And your record producer would agree, I believe, or he would not have shot such a deeply arousing film in the desert with you.'

'Chris has a commercial mind and the money to produce any of his visions as he chooses to——'

'Visions!' drawled the sheikh. 'Another word for fantasy. And every art-form since the dawn of time has been composed of fantasy, *bint*, as you well know.'

'Your interest in me is hardly artistic,' she said thickly, 'as you well know!'

The dark eyes flicked slowly, indolently, to her mouth. 'Ah,' he said softly and his eyes grew intent, 'but it could be, my Sheba. It could be...'

Dry-mouthed, intolerably attracted to him, she said, 'Not if it is forced on me!'

'And there lies the beauty,' he said, gaze flicking intently to her breasts, taut and swollen with arousal beneath the gold caftan, 'because woman surrenders to man: not the other way around. And you, my Sheba, will eventually come to see the beauty in that, for it is the only truth between the sexes, and one you must acknowledge if you are to be my Sheba.'

'Sheba...' she said. 'Who is Sheba and why do you——?'

'We will eat now.' The sheikh clapped his hands, and at once three servants emerged from a tent, carrying trays on which were many domed dishes, coffee-pots, filigree cups, brass plates and a thousand different scents of herbs and spices assailing her nostrils and making her stomach clench in hunger.

The dishes were placed on the trestle-table and Bethsheba looked angrily at Suliman's hard profile, hating him for refusing to answer her repeated questions about Sheba. Surely she had a right to know? The lids were removed from the brass dishes. She saw hot chunks of meat in rich, spicy sauces, and thick hunks of bread, and her mouth watered.

'Eat,' Suliman said, pushing her plate towards her.

'I'm not hungry!' she said angrily, rebellion in her eyes. She would die rather than take anything from this arrogant desert prince.

'Come!' He frowned. 'You are ravenous. Admit it and eat.'

Her eyes flashed angrily to his face. 'I'd rather die than eat anything you put before me!'

'Out here,' he said coolly, 'death is always imminent unless one is on one's guard. I would not joke about it so carelessly, *bint*, lest it should claim you for your foolish pride and arrogance.'

'Arrogance!' She stared, furious. 'How dare you even mention it in connection with me after what you've——?'

'Is it not arrogance to believe the dove can defeat the hawk?' he asked softly.

Her face flushed. 'I'm a woman and you're a man! Please drop the Arabian proverbs and hyperbole!'

'Sheba,' he said harshly, 'when it is time I shall remind you most forcefully of the differences in our sexes! Until then, I advise you to think only of yourself and your well-being and eat!'

'I will not eat!' she said furiously, hating him. It seemed the only power left to her—the power to refuse to eat, and she wasn't going to give it up without a fight, however stupid.

'You are proud, Sheba. But your pride will be conquered—of that I assure you.'

'Stop talking of conquering me,' she burst out, trembling, 'of mastering me, taming me, dominating me——'

'Your eyes flare with excitement,' he said, laughing softly, 'and your face is flushed with fever. If I felt your pulse now—what would I find?'

'I'm angry!' she said, snatching her hand away before he could take it and feel her thudding pulsation. 'I have every right to be angry!'

'And every right to know the ecstasy of submission to a man.'

She caught her breath, staring as the camp-fires flickered across the planes of that hard, handsome face.

'Your body is made for love,' said the sheikh, 'yet it receives none. You are hungry, yet in foolish pride you refuse food. Tell me, Sheba—why do you deny your own needs?'

'I . . .' she was breathless, staring '. . . I don't . . .'

'You saw me in the desert,' he said under his breath, 'and you saw yourself in my arms, forced to yield to my kisses and my touch.'

'Lies!' she whispered, mouth dry. 'Lies . . .'

'Now you close the doors of your mind,' his hand moved to her hair, then to her throat, stroking her to the pulse-beat as she stared, lips parted, 'and you deny your need for love, your need for food, and your need for fulfilment. I say to you: end these denials. Take what you need. Feed your every desire and end your own starvation!'

Unable to speak, she felt her gaze lock deeper with his, and, as his fingers stroked their farewell on her tense, throbbing neck, she was forced to realise that what he said was true—she was hungry, ravenously hungry, and yet she stupidly refused to eat.

'So.' Suliman turned from her, pushed her dish slowly back in front of her. 'You will eat now and forget your pride, hmm?'

She stared down at the food and said thickly, 'Very well.'

He smiled, his fingers left her throat, and he turned to eat too.

Bethsheba tore a slice of bread and dipped it into the thick, dark spicy sauce. The flavour exploded on her tongue, and she closed her eyes, surrendering to her hunger as warmth and energy flowed into her body and relaxed her a little.

But tonight, she told herself, when the camp is dark I will steal a horse and escape. She ate hungrily, the thick chunks of meat delicious, and the barbaric freedom of dipping bread in sauce enjoyable.

'Fulfillment is satisfying indeed, is it not, Sheba?' asked Suliman beside her, and she turned her head, like a thief caught red-handed, to stare at him in the firelight and feel the dark flush of secret desire steal over her skin.

'I was hungry,' she said thickly.

'And so you ate.'

'Yes, I ate!' she broke out hotly. 'What's wrong with that?'

The dark eyes glittered with satisfaction. 'Nothing, *bint*. Nothing at all.'

His meaning was not lost on her and she hated him for it, hated him for knowing how she felt when he . . . Her eyes closed as that dark passion pulsated through her body and she thought feverishly, I have to get away!

After dinner, the sheikh said, 'Come. It is a pleasant night. Let us walk.'

Bethsheba rose obediently to her feet, the bells at her wrists and ankles jangling softly, the symbols of her captivity fastened there by her new master. Resentment burned in her.

They walked together across the soft, cool sands, away from the tent and moving among the Bedouin who lounged around the camp-fires, talking. The murmured words of Arabic were strangely seductive to her ears as she walked beside the sheikh, heard his people speak respectfully to him, heard him reply in deep tones of authority, and realised anew how much power he truly held.

'You were born here, weren't you?' Bethsheba asked as they rounded the last tent and the sickle moon glowed beside the diamond stars above. 'Not at the palace, but here—in the desert.'

'Yes.' He looked at her with some surprise, dark brows lifting. 'How did you guess that?'

'I don't know . . .' She smiled slightly. 'Maybe because you seem more at home here—more real than you did at Agadir.'

'I see.' A slight smile touched the hard mouth. He studied the sands as he walked, hands behind his back, the dark blue caftan heightening his masculinity as he moved. 'Well, you are right, *bint*. I was indeed born in the desert, and brought up here, too.'

'Why?' she asked, intrigued.

The hooded eyes flicked to her coolly. 'Because it was written.'

'Kismet again!' she said resentfully. 'I suppose you believe everything is written!'

'You do not?'

'Of course not! We make our own destinies! Man's fate lies not in the stars, as Shakespeare said—and I agree with him.'

'Yet Shakespeare's was a great and powerful destiny,' Suliman said coolly, 'and who among us can say it was not part of Allah's great plan?'

She smiled, gold eyes amused as they met his. 'Shakespeare didn't believe in Allah!'

He laughed deeply. 'We each have our own god.'

Bethsheba's smile remained, and she looked down at the cool sands as they walked, enjoying the feel of it beneath her soft-slippered feet, and aware that she was also enjoying Suliman's company far more than she would admit.

'And you, Sheba?' Suliman asked. 'Were you born in London?'

'No.' She shook her golden head.

'Good. I cannot imagine the child Sheba playing in concrete canyons.'

She laughed, looking up, eyes dancing. 'That's clever of you! As a matter of fact, I'm what they call an army brat. My father was a brigadier in the British army, and my mother an army wife.'

'You were born in England, then? In a sleepy little village with green lawns and afternoon tea and——'

'No, I was born in Bahrain.'

He stopped walking.

Bethsheba went on a step or two, then stopped, turning to look at his dark, powerful silhouette framed against that desert night sky of brilliant diamond light.

'Bahrain?' he asked thickly, staring. 'You were born in Arabia?'

'Yes!' she said as her blood began to throb with strange excitement. 'I lived there until I was five years old.'

He stared at her fixedly, dark eyes glittering; then he was moving towards her, gripping her arms with strong hands. 'You tell me this, yet you deny your destiny!'

Breathless, she struggled against his male strength. 'Yes, but what difference can it possibly make to——?'

'It makes a great deal of difference, *bint*,' he said harshly, 'as you are about to find out!' And he whirled her around, his strong fingers around her wrists as he pulled her to the royal tent.

'What are you doing?' she demanded hoarsely, struggling, sand flying around her belled ankles as she fought him.

'I am giving you your first lesson!' he said as he thrust her into the tent. 'Your first glimpse of the ecstasy of submission!'

'Oh, God...!' she whispered, stumbling back from him, body pulsing with a desire that appalled her as she was overwhelmed by him, pushed back on to the silk cushions though she cried out, jewelled slippers tumbling off slender feet, the bells on her wrists and ankles jangling as she fell and the scent of burning cassia oil filling her with evocative sensual memories.

'Born in Arabia,' Suliman said thickly, his body on hers as they fell, 'with hair of gold and skin the colour of a sand-cat!'

'Don't!' she burst out hotly, struggling beneath him.

'You will admit your desire, *bint*!' he said tightly, jerking her face round to meet his as they sprawled together on the cushions. 'You will admit it and submit to your master!'

'No!'

His dark eyes flashed. 'And I say you will!' Then his head swooped, and that hard mouth closed over hers in a passionate kiss that made her gasp, moaning under the onslaught of unleashed desire, her whole body arching towards him as his tongue invaded her mouth and the hunger flared out of her as she opened her mouth beneath his.

Moaning, head flung back, she gasped as he moved his burning mouth from hers, sliding it down over her throat to find the throbbing pulse he knew was there.

'Stop it!' Bethsheba whispered thickly, clutching his dark head, too weak to push him away, too weak to hold him close. 'Stop...!'

'Tell me you want me!' he said harshly under his breath, his mouth at her throat. 'Tell me and submit!'

'Go to hell!' she said wildly, heart thudding, and then caught her breath as his strong hand tugged down the bodice of her caftan to reveal her bare breast, springing into view, her pink nipple hard and engorged with need. 'Oh, God, don't...don't...' she whispered thickly as he stroked it with one finger, making her burn with heated desire. 'Don't!'

'Submit!' he said thickly, and slid one strong thigh between hers, splaying her, helpless, beneath him.

She stared at him in a hot grip of fever and hatred, breathing erratically, her heartbeat drumming beneath his strong hand as it lay motionless against her breast.

'So be it,' Suliman said softly, and smiled as he lowered his head to her breast.

Bethsheba started to struggle but he pinned her arms above her head. His mouth fastened on her breast and she gave a low, hoarse moan, closing her eyes, gasping as he sucked hungrily at her nipple, his strong thigh moving in slow rhythmic motions between hers until she felt as though she were no longer flesh and blood but hot, molten lava to be moulded at his command, her body moving against his in blind response to that drumming, drugging rhythm, her eyes closed and her head back, reeling in hot sensuality.

When his hand moved to her thigh she felt common sense flood back to her along with fear, and the panic as he pushed her caftan up to bare her thigh made her jackknife against him with a startled cry.

'No!' She struggled to be free of those pinning hands, her eyes wild. 'Please!'

He studied her fixedly, eyes burning, breathing harshly, nostrils flaring with a desire that terrified her as she looked into those black eyes and saw an answering fire of dark passion.

'I'm frightened, Suliman!' she broke out hoarsely, truthfully. 'Frightened...this is madness...I can't do it!'

There was a tense silence. He was fighting for self-restraint, his body tense and she heard him take control over his breathing first before he spoke.

'It is a madness we both feel, Sheba.' His voice in fever was thickly accented in Arabic. 'Do not

deny what is in your soul, or your soul will deny
you—and that is a hell I would not wish on my
worst enemy.'

Her eyes closed to shut out the dark truth in his
eyes. 'I can't!' she said hoarsely. 'I just can't!' Tears
sprang blinding-hot to her eyes and she struggled
not to show them, but they squeezed out beneath
her closed lids and slid down each temple to drop
upon the cushions.

His hands released her wrists, he covered her
breasts, and then the strong arms were around her,
pulling her tight against his hard chest, holding her
tousled blonde head against the thud of his
passionate heart.

'Hush,' he said deeply, 'no tears in a lovers' bed.
Lovemaking is the sweetest pleasure—even the pain
must be sweet.'

'I'm so afraid!' she whispered huskily into his
warm chest. 'I should never have let you see what
was in my mind, Suliman! It was folly...'

'Ah...' his soft voice taunted, 'you admit it,
then?'

Shame burnt her face. 'You knew...you knew
all along!'

He laughed under his breath. 'I saw it in your
eyes, *bint*. That first day in the desert. And in the
tension of your body as I rode up.'

'It wasn't deliberate!' she said hoarsely. 'It wasn't
conscious!'

'I saw that, too,' he said softly, his head fitting
perfectly above hers as he held her close. 'You have
the face of a virgin and the body of a she-cat. A
potent mix, for any man. To tame such a woman...'
his arms tightened possessively around her
'...makes my head spin with such desire! Makes
my blood throb to the beat of a powerful drum.

And makes my body——' he slowly pressed his hardness against her lower belly '—yours!'

'But you don't understand——' she began fearfully.

'I understand perfectly,' he cut in. 'You accepted the challenge in my eyes and the destiny I offered you, but as a virgin you are too afraid to fulfil it.'

'I never at any time accepted——'

'You are here, *bint*,' he said deeply. 'Behold—destiny is upon you.'

Slowly, silently, Bethsheba drew back to look into that hard royal face, and her heart skipped beats in the silence as she tried and failed to deny in her heart what he said.

'You understand me, Sheba,' Suliman said deeply, 'do you not?'

'What choice do I have?' she said bitterly, fighting her desire.

'Good.' He nodded, eyes moving slowly over her face. 'Then tonight we sleep on our understanding, and tomorrow...we leave for the Great Palace of Suliman!'

'What...?' she stared, appalled. 'But—but I thought you wanted to stay here!'

'No,' he said, mouth hard. 'When your moment of surrender comes, Sheba, it will be in the palace of my ancestors, as it is written.'

'I won't let you do it!' she protested fiercely, pushing back from him, both hands on his hard chest, determination glittering in her gold eyes. 'I won't let you take me there and I won't let you——'

'You will do as you are told, *bint*,' he said flatly, eyes narrowing, 'and go where you are taken.' He got to his feet, face hard and determined, and strode to the tent entrance, turning to look back at her over one broad shoulder. 'Rest well tonight, Sheba, for tomorrow we ride for the palace of my ancestors—and the fulfilment of our destiny!'

He swept the tent flap aside and strode out, leaving Bethsheba staring after him, eyes filled with fear and anger, hands clenched with impotent fury as those words rang in her ears.

I won't let this happen to me! she told herself fiercely. I must do something, I must!

The camp was asleep by one o'clock. Bethsheba had paced the tent for hours, listening to the movements of the *douar*, her ears attuned to every sound.

When at last all was silent she slipped out of the royal tent. The camp-fires were all out; all but one, and a guard sat propped against a palm tree beside it, a rifle in his hands.

Bethsheba refused to be stopped by one guard! Determinedly, she removed her slippers and inched forward, her eyes flicking tensely between the guard and the row of horses tethered to oasis trees at the edge of the encampment.

The guard did not move. Suddenly she realised he was asleep, and relief flooded her as she moved quickly, silently, to the tethered horses. They were bare-backed, so she looked around for some saddles.

No saddles.

Her heart sank in despair. No saddles! How on earth would she manage? She had never ridden bareback before and—but yes, she had! The sickle moon seemed to smile at her as memory flashed in her mind and she thought of Bahrain...

When she was a small child in Bahrain there had been a large horse-enclosure close to the Brigadier's—her father's—house. Bethsheba had often ridden bareback, defying convention and making her father roar furiously after her to come back as she rode, fearless and free, into the desert.

I was fearless, once, she thought; but where was that fearlessness now? Eroded by adult life, by tragedy and desperation. Helpless little songbirds who had to sing for their supper could do no more than face the daily challenge of a microphone, a new medley and twenty lengths before breakfast.

Her mouth tightened with grim determination. Moving silently among the horses, she found the honey-gold horse that Suliman had given her to ride here with him. OK, she had no saddle, but she did have reins, she did have courage, and she did have a very good reason for getting away from here! If Suliman took her to his palace in the Sahara tomorrow he would have her in his bed before sunset, and she could not let that happen.

Bethsheba led the honey horse out and across the sand at a very slow pace. She could not risk waking the *douar* guard or causing any kind of commotion. Once she was a good six hundred yards from the edge of the camp she took a deep breath, stepped back a few paces, then ran at the horse as she had done as a child in Bahrain, and leapt on to its back.

Joy flooded her as she landed perfectly astride the horse. Excitement flashed in her eyes as she took the reins, nudged the horse straight into a fast trot, then slid it effortlessly into canter and felt the wind in her hair.

It felt so good to ride bareback! The slits in the sides of her gold caftan bared her long legs as they gripped the horse, her body moving in perfect harmony with its long-legged strides. The goat-hair tents of the sheikh's *douar* receded into the night behind her, and she went into gallop.

A fast gallop. The wind was in her hair, the time flashed by, and still she rode, sweat dewing her cool skin as she bent to the horse and miles were eaten up by the fast, beautiful stallion.

She rode for hours. Dawn began to seep across the landscape, turning the sands lilac. She checked her water-bottles. The dawn was moving relentlessly, and the sands were fast turning pale gold as warmth seeped into the desert.

Soon it was sunrise: and sunrise brought danger. The sun was burning on her golden head now, sweat covering her flesh and that of the horse as they galloped into the furnace-heat of the desert morning. Sand flew from its hoofs, the shadow of a hawk soared in a piercingly blue sky above, and a sandcat slunk out from beneath the shade of animals' bones.

She was tiring; so was her horse. It was so hot, the sands so endless. Bethsheba knew she would have to stop and rest at the next opportunity—she didn't want the horse breaking down in exhaustion.

When she saw the shimmer of green on the horizon she gasped in relief, then told herself it was a mirage. But, as the horse headed instinctively for the waters of an oasis, Bethsheba realised it was no mirage: she had found sanctuary.

After riding like mad towards it she leapt off her horse as they reached the lush waters and greenery. The horse drank greedily, thirstily, and Bethsheba slithered, trembling, to the water's edge, sinking her face and hair into the water, drinking thirstily, gasping for breath as the cool clear water drenched her burning head and hair and cooled her.

When she had drunk her fill she slumped, exhausted, against the rough-diamond bark of a palm tree. It was so beautiful here. Her wet lashes closed lightly...she was so tired. But she must not rest! She had to reach a town, a telephone, and safety!

Glancing at her horse, she saw it rested quietly in the shade of a cactus. A sigh broke her lips. They were both exhausted. Perhaps it would be best to stay out of the dangerous sun until later.

Slowly, sleep began to claim her, though she fought against it...

CHAPTER FIVE

HORSES' hoofs woke her. Jerking awake, Bethsheba stared across the gold sands as though in a dream to see a thunder of desert warriors approaching on horseback.

In a flash, she leapt up, running for her horse. It whinnied and danced away from her, leaving her crying out in fear, her gold hair flashing in the sun as she turned to see the warriors and see, suddenly, with heart-stopping fear, excitement and relief, their leader.

Suliman's white robes gleamed in the sunlight, the white head-dress and gold *iqal* symbolising his authority. He rode with his men, and there were twenty of them, all in dark robes and turbans, carrying spears and guns, their horses black, brown and dun.

Suddenly, his men halted. Only Suliman himself galloped up to the oasis, and his dark eyes flashed in his hard, arrogant face as he bore down on her in a storm of sand.

'You ran from me!' he bit out under his breath, and the stallion danced beneath him, sand kicking up from its hoofs.

'I had to!' Bethsheba raised her head with courage, trembling before him but refusing to show it. 'I had to run, and I will do it again if you take me back!'

He took the long black whip from his saddle. 'You leave me no choice, then!'

67

She stared, taking a step back. 'For God's sake!'

'My men are watching!' he bit out, lips drawing back in a snarl. 'Do you want me to be humiliated before them?'

'But you can't——'

He raised the whip in one savage hand. It cracked the air as it soared in a vicious arc before lashing the sand by her bare feet. 'I will teach you obedience, Sheba!'

'No!' Breathless, she turned to run, but he followed her, and that long black whip cracked curled out again and again as his horse rode after her while she ran for her own horse a few feet away.

'Don't get on that horse!' the sheikh bit out. 'Don't, you little fool!'

'I'm not staying here to be whipped into obedience by you!' Bethsheba broke out furiously, gasping as her sweaty trembling hands fumbled with the stiff mane and lost their hold.

'Don't get on it!' The sheikh circled her, whip raised. 'You'll force me to really use the whip on you!'

'Go to hell!' Bethsheba hauled herself on to the gold horse.

But her balance was shot to pieces, and she slipped, falling to the ground, heart pounding as she found herself lying on her back in the sand staring up at Suliman.

He dismounted. Oxblood leather riding boots sent sand flying as he landed, white robes billowing out, to stride towards her like a legend, the whip in his right hand.

'Don't...!' Bethsheba begged hoarsely, barefoot, on her back, one slender thigh bared by the slits in the gold caftan.

He towered over her, his face implacable. 'Scream!' he bit out thickly, and the whip lashed the sand inches from her bare thigh.

She wriggled away from the stinging tip, gasping, 'Please . . .!'

'Scream!' he commanded, and the whip cracked again, missing her thigh by a hair's breadth, and, when she stared into his face and the whip cracked again, she suddenly understood.

She screamed.

Suliman's hard mouth flickered with a smile. His eyes flashed with satisfaction as the whip rose and fell for all to see while Bethsheba screamed and writhed in simulated pain.

Suddenly the whip was thrown aside.

'Enough!' Suliman said under his breath and stepped forward, going down on one knee to slide strong arms around her. She went into his arms without a struggle, burying her face in his strong neck and breathing in the scents she had longed for even as she'd fled: the scent of his skin, his maleness, the scent of horseflesh and leather and the East.

'Thank you,' she said huskily into his throat.

'You should not have fled,' he said deeply, and drew back to look at her with hard dark eyes. 'I would not have forced you to make love with me. Did I not make that clear, *bint*?'

'Never!' she said, meeting that dark gaze with courage. 'But I did make it clear that I wanted to be returned to my home. And that I did not want to make love with—— Oh!' She broke off with a gasp as his strong hand curved over her breast.

'But you do want to make love with me,' he said under his breath, one finger stroking the erect unfettered nipple beneath the gold silk, enjoying the dark flush that stole into her cheeks. 'Admit it and find fulfilment.'

'Admit it and find myself used!' she said hoarsely, heart hammering at his touch. 'You don't care about me, Suliman! You only want to——'

'So do you, *bint*!' he said thickly, and suddenly his hard mouth was covering hers, silencing her with a kiss that made her blood sing and her body weaken with dark heat, passion stirring a response in her that was terrifyingly wanton.

Distant laughter and a ripple of applause reached her ears, and pride rose angrily in her, making her fight him, hands pushing at his broad shoulders. He trapped her struggling arms behind her back easily, and his mouth ravaged hers, pushing her body back against the sand, his own body pinning it there as he kissed her to within an inch of her life, leaving her shuddering with excitement and anger.

When he raised his head he studied her flushed, fevered face with satisfaction and said thickly, 'I will conquer you, she-cat, and turn your bites and scratches into the marks of love!'

'Never!' she breathed thickly, hating him, eyes wild in her fevered face. 'Never!'

'Your passionate refusals only stir my blood more,' he said under his breath, and then he was lifting her, standing straight and tall as he swung her into his arms and strode towards his horse, amused by the mocking laughter of his men who acknowledged his very obvious success with this gold-skinned she-cat who was his to tame.

Bethsheba could do nothing but fume with silent rage as the sheikh lifted her on to his white stallion and mounted behind her. His strong arms held her in front of him as he took the reins and nudged the powerful steed into a fast canter.

Excitement filled her as they rode across the desert, the sheikh leading his warriors. The cluster of Arabian horses thundered across the sands; spears raised, guns raised, a banner flying in scarlet and gold as the sheikh led them at a fast gallop, his white head-dress and robes flying behind him, and the honey-gold horse Bethsheba had escaped on alongside, riderless but still a member of the Auda Khazir.

I'm almost pleased to have been caught, she realised with incredulity. Her excited eyes were flicking from side to side as the wind rippled the Audi Khazir banner, and she breathed in the scent of a warrior race and their sheikh.

When the *douar* finally came in sight again, it was late afternoon. The heat shimmered on the horizon, making the goat-hair tents wave like a mirage.

The sheikh called something in Arabic, laughing as he rode his horse up to the royal tent. His people clustered round, laughing, looking at Bethsheba knowingly, and she flushed with hot colour as she met their gazes, lifting her gold head proudly.

The sheikh dismounted and turned, strong hands catching her waist as he lifted her down from the horse. He snapped his fingers, issued a command to a servant, and took Bethsheba's arm to lead her forcibly into the royal tent.

'Now, *bint*!' he said tightly as he thrust her into the tent. 'You will explain to me your reasons for leaving!'

'But I thought I——' she began, flustered, stepping back from him.

'You ran from me!' he bit out, dark eyes blazing suddenly with rage—the rage he had kept hidden from her in the desert but which now poured out in no uncertain terms. 'You ran from me? From all of this? From the dream I brought to life for you!'

'This isn't a dream!' she said hotly, struggling to cope with this new side of him, this hot black rage that made her heart stop beating as she faced him in the dim gold light of the royal tent. 'I'm your prisoner, with no rights of my own and no hope of freedom!'

'You want this!' he said bitingly. 'You want all of this!' He gestured angrily around at the silk cushions, cassia lamps, shiraz rugs. 'You want everything I can give you; from my love to my world and my desert!'

'I don't!' she spat, hating him. 'Not like this! Not kidnapped and held prisoner and whipped into obedience by you like a——'

'The whip did not touch you!'

'You humiliated me in front of your men!'

'I am their sheikh!' he bit out, striding angrily towards her, eyes flashing. 'And you are my woman! In their eyes and in mine—you will obey me or pay the consequences!'

She backed angrily. 'I'm not your woman!' she spat. 'You had to kidnap me to get me here—that makes me your prisoner, not your——'

'Little bitch!' His hands shot out forcefully, gripping her upper arms and dragging her towards him even as she struggled. 'So—you are not my woman! You are an innocent kidnap-victim! A poor helpless female being forced to respond to my un-wanted attentions!'

'That's right!' she said bitterly, struggling, eyes flashing vivid gold as she fought him with fierce fury and hatred. 'I am an innocent victim of your——'

'And you don't welcome my touch?' he bit out thickly, pinning her hands suddenly behind her back, his fingers clasping them there like handcuffs.

'You're a barbarian!' she flung hotly, shaking, fighting him even as her heart pounded with fierce arousal and excitement. 'A savage! A vile, unspeakable——'

'Yes?' he cut in harshly, and tugged aside the bodice of her caftan to reveal her full, swollen breast, the rose-beige nipple engorged and erect.

'Take your filthy hands off me...' she whispered thickly, twisting from that all-seeing gaze and the humiliation of having her fierce desire revealed to him.

His eyes flashed with anger. 'You want me, *bint*! Admit it or——'

'Let me go!' she burst out fiercely, fighting him.

'Admit it!' His nostrils flared. 'Tell me what you feel! Say it out loud and have done with these lies!'

'Never!'

'You will say it, Sheba!' he bit out roughly, and his anger vibrated between them, dominating her suddenly, even as she fought him, her heart thudding a powerful rhythm as she felt the power balance swing overpoweringly in his favour, as it had been from the beginning.

He was pushing her backwards, on to the silk cushions, and as she fell with him she was breathing hectically, pushing at him, desperate to escape the fierce desire that clawed at her.

'No...' she was whispering thickly. 'No...no...'

But her body told a different story, and as his hard mouth closed over hers, as his hands pinned her wrists above her head, she heard herself moan in helpless arousal.

He was pushing her lips apart, and as his tongue slid in to meet hers she closed her eyes, opened her mouth beneath his and dark passion flooded her.

'You want me,' he taunted softly, his eyes mocking as he ravished her mouth with expert sensuality, and as his strong hand moved back to cover her bared breast she sucked in her breath, arching against him as his fingers found her erect nipple, and her blood-pressure rocketed through the roof.

'Don't . . .' she was breathing thickly, twisting beneath him, heart hammering as she struggled to retain consciousness, 'don't . . . don't . . .'

'Tell me yes!' he bit out, and bent his commanding head. As his hot mouth fastened over her nipple she heard herself draw in her breath like a drowning woman, struggling against those iron hands that held her, her heart drumming ferociously.

'Stop it!' she whispered thickly, hating him, loving him, excited beyond bearing by that hard, hot mouth. 'I hate it when you——'

'You will tell me, Sheba,' he cut in raggedly, and bared her other breast with a swift, ruthless hand, covering it, watching her flushed and excited face as he stroked her to fever-pitch, 'or I will have you now!'

'No!' she denied hotly, then gasped on a hoarse note of intolerable excitement as his strong hand moved down, moved to her thigh bared by the slit in her caftan.

'Tell me you want me!' he said hoarsely, and covered her mouth in a draining, drugging kiss. His strong hand pushed at the caftan while she writhed beneath him. 'Tell me you want me!' he said against her throbbing throat. 'Tell me this is what you long for too! Tell me! Tell me . . .!'

'Oh, Suliman, please . . . please!' she begged hotly, and cried out in hoarse pleasure as his strong hand pushed the silken golden caftan up to her waist, sliding his strong thigh between hers and making her arch against him in hot, molten desire.

'Tell me you want me!' he bit out thickly, his heart thundering like a hammer. 'Tell me quickly, or I'll take you, Sheba, I swear I'll take you . . .'

'Yes!' she whispered in terrified excitement, clutching his muscled shoulders, her mouth moving hotly against his. 'I'll say anything . . .'

'The truth!' he said hoarsely, desire like black fire in his eyes. 'Tell me the truth! That you wanted me when you first saw me! That you wanted this to happen!'

'Yes!' she moaned, throbbing like wildfire as she lay sprawled beneath him. 'Yes!'

'Say it out loud for me to hear clearly!' he bit out thickly.

'I wanted you when I first saw you!' she whispered against his hard, hot, insistent mouth. 'I wanted this to happen! I wanted it . . . oh, yes . . . yes . . . and I still want it!'

With a hoarse cry of triumph he captured her mouth again, and this time the kiss he gave her was so passionate that she almost blacked out with pleasure.

Blindly, she clutched at his muscled shoulders with shaking hands, and suddenly the desire overwhelmed her as she allowed herself to touch his chest, to touch him at last, to feel the heartbeat that pulsed blood around his body, to push the dark jerkin aside and touch the thick black hairs on his chest, and heard his fierce, rough sounds of pleasure as he shifted above her, his body passionate.

Suddenly a commotion outside began to filter through to them.

Breathing raggedly, the shiekh lifted his head.

'What is it?' Bethsheba whispered jerkily, blinking, reluctant to leave that honeyed, vibrant intimacy.

They could hear the men shouting outside, running about as horses whinnied, and the sound of...

'A helicopter!' the shiekh bit out under his breath.

She met his startled gaze with a jolt. 'Chris!'

'Damn him!' Suliman swore thickly. 'He's come for you! Will you go with him?'

Unable to breathe or speak, she just stared at him, confused.

'Will you go with him?' he demanded fiercely, gripping her shoulders and staring down at her with blazing eyes.

What choice did she have? Of course she would go with Chris! but she knew better than to tell Suliman that! He would rage and try to re-kidnap her. So she just looked into those dark, powerful eyes and said nothing.

'If you won't answer me that,' Suliman said thickly, mouth biting out the words, 'you will at least tell me the truth of what you just admitted! Did you mean it? What you just said, Sheba! Did you speak truly?'

The helicopter blades were vibrating above the royal tent, sending its cloth walls into a fury of a sandstorm.

'Yes!' Bethsheba whispered, safe now, about to escape him forever, and able, suddenly, in her

moment of freedom, to admit her fierce desire. 'I—
I wanted you when I first saw you! I shared this,
your fantasy, all along.'

There was a tense silence. A hard smile touched
his mouth. Suddenly he released her, discarding her
as though she was a toy, and strode to the tent flap,
sweeping it aside and striding out with a backward
glance.

Bethsheba sat up, eyes flashing with outrage and
indignation. How dared he? Anger flooded her and
her face burnt with humiliation. He forced me to
admit my most secret desires, and then he tossed
me aside as though I were a doll!

Hating him bitterly, hating herself more, she
dragged herself outside the tent, shaking with
emotion. The helicopter was landing, blades
flashing in the sunlight as sand flew everywhere and
the goat-hair tents billowed, and the horses danced
and whinnied in fright.

The helicopter bounced lightly on the sands. The
sheikh was walking towards it, white robes billowing out around his powerful frame. The helicopter door flashed open.

Chris Burton stepped on to the sand, blond hair
gleaming, dressed in faded blue jeans and white
shirt, tall and golden and classically handsome;
Apollo incarnate, his mind filled with Shakespeare,
the Beatles and dreams of glory.

'Chris!' Bethsheba cried, and ran towards him
to fling herself into the security of his arms.

Suliman's eyes flashed with jealous rage as he
stared at her, his hard mouth tight with anger, but
Bethsheba didn't care—he deserved it for having
thrown her aside so casually after using her like
that.

'Beth, I've been frantic!' Chris was saying. 'What on earth possessed you——?'

'A crazy impulse!' she sobbed into his throat.

'But don't you realise what could have happened to you?'

'She was under my protection!' The sheikh's commanding voice rang out. 'She came to no harm.'

Chris looked up angrily, Bethsheba in his arms. 'She's worth millions! She's a major star with hundreds of people depending on her! I can't just have her wandering off into the desert like this! For all I knew, she'd been kidnapped, and I could have had a ransom note demanding money that——'

'You must be tired after your long search,' the sheikh cut in flatly. 'May I offer you some refreshment? A chance to rest?'

'You must be joking!' Chris was angry at being cut off by the powerful desert chief. 'I'm taking Beth straight back to——'

'Your pilot is tired,' Suliman interrupted, his face coolly arrogant; 'I will offer him some mint tea before he flies back to Tangier.'

'Now just a minute!' Chris said, furious, as the sheikh strode past him. 'I've got a lot more to say before I——'

Sheikh Suliman turned, his hawk-like face arrogant. 'You may speak with Sheba in the privacy of the royal tent. Tea will be brought to you.'

The helicopter pilot had got out now and was walking towards the sheikh, his dark-skinned Arabic face filled with respect as he salaamed.

'Well,' Chris muttered angrily, 'I guess I can spare another hour.'

'You will be back in Tangier tonight,' said the sheikh. 'I have matters to attend to. You will excuse me.' He turned on the heel of his riding boot and strode away, his men following him as he spoke to the pilot.

'I could easily come to blows with that guy,' Chris said under his breath. 'He really is the archetypal arrogant desert prince, isn't he?'

'Yes.' Bethsheba's eyes flashed gold fire as she studied Suliman.

'Come on, then,' Chris gave a deep sigh, 'lead me to this royal tent. We've got some talking to do.'

They moved across the sands. Bethsheba's feet were still bare, and her gold hair tousled from Suliman's lovemaking. She pushed aside the tent flap and went in, followed by Chris.

'Good God!' Chris stopped short inside the tent. 'This is sensational, Beth...like something out of the *Arabian Nights*!'

'Yes...' Her eyes slid around the luxury she had become accustomed to.

'Well, I can see why you leapt at the chance to come here.' Chris tapped a gold filigree lamp, smelt the cassia oil, then bent to finger a silk cushion. 'What an incredible place!'

'Like something out of a fantasy...'

Her softly spoken words clung to the air, and Chris turned slowly, staring at her as though he had never seen her before, eyes racing over her from her tousled hair to her full mouth, bruised from the sheikh's kisses, the sudden blaze of sensuality in her eyes and body, the gold caftan falling in rich silk over her obviously bare breasts.

'A fantasy?' Chris asked.

She flushed. 'Well, it is, isn't it?'

He dropped the cushion, unsmiling. 'What's happened here, Beth?'

Hot colour swept her face. 'Nothing's happened!'

'Then why are you talking like this? Looking like——' He bit back the words, ran a hand through his blond hair. 'You don't look like Beth any more. Something's . . . changed in you.'

Accepting it without denial, she said huskily, 'Is that so awful?'

'Did I say it was?'

'You made it sound awful!' she said angrily, shame sweeping her.

'Well . . . I'm just thinking of your career. Your fans. Beth—your image is perfect right now. Young, golden, innocent and healthy. Teenage girls flock to you because you represent everything they want to be.' He shrugged. 'You know what they say— never change a winning formula.'

'I'm not a formula!' She lifted her head angrily. 'I'm a woman!'

'I didn't say you were a formula, I just——' He broke off, staring again, then said suddenly, 'What's happened out here, Beth? You've changed completely!'

'In a few hours?' she asked, shaken. 'Don't be absurd!'

'It's that sheikh, isn't it? He's done this to you!'

Scarlet colour burned her face. 'I don't know what you mean.'

Chris's eyes widened, and into the tent stole the tension of realisation. 'He's made love to you!' he whispered, pale.

'No!' She turned away, the guilt in her eyes too revealing. How had he known? How could he have guessed? There had only been a few kisses . . . but so much fire; so much passion.

'I'm right!' Chris said under his breath, fists clenching. 'That bastard...!'

The tent flap was swept aside. A servant in white turban and jellaba entered with a tray of mint tea and spicy biscuits. He laid it on the trestle-table, then left with a bow.

'I'll pour the tea, shall I?' Bethsheba asked shakily, desperate to change the subject, stop Chris probing, end the whole upsetting discussion. 'You must be very thirsty.' She moved past him to the table, pouring hot mint tea into filigree cups.

Chris moved towards her. The fury in his face was almost as bad as the accusation in his eyes. Bethsheba felt a flash of anger with him, but she pushed it aside guiltily.

'Here.' She smiled tensely as she offered him his tea, then took her own and lay back on the silk cushions, watching him through gold lashes.

'My God,' Chris said softly, staring down at her, 'you're completely at home.'

She looked up guiltily.

'It's as though you belong here.'

'Don't be absurd——' she began huskily, putting her tea down on the table.

'You know it as well as I do!' Chris said thickly. 'And I'm right! That bastard Suliman has made love to you!'

'Chris——'

'He has!' Chris put his cup down angrily, mint tea spilling on the arabesque table. 'He's made love to you and destroyed everything that was so precious about you!'

'You're jumping to conclusions that——'

'Don't lie to me!' Chris knelt on the silk cushions, staring at her. 'It was what made you so special...that innocence...like a ravishing bloom in a glass case, never touched or crushed or plucked...'

She caught her breath, shocked. 'Chris!'

'You were so damned sexy,' he said hoarsely, 'but you didn't know it! You had no idea! You thought you were the girl next door, but all the time you were Lolita, luring men on without meaning to, making them——'

'Oh, God...'

'But now you know!' Chris said furiously. 'Now you know just how sexy you are, and that bastard Suliman has made you aware of it! He's turned my perfect little teenager into a woman and I'd like to——'

'I'm not a teenager any more!' she broke out fiercely. 'I'm——'

'You'll always be a teenager to your fans!' Chris exploded. 'All those little thirteen-year-old wannabees out there—do you think they wannabee what you are now? The sheikh's mistress?'

Her eyes flashed with gold fury. 'I am not his mistress!'

'You will be,' he snapped back, 'if you stay in this damned desert a second longer with that bastard Suliman!'

'He hasn't made love to me, Chris! I swear it!'

'Beth!' he said fiercely, and suddenly swept her into his arms, holding her so tight that she could barely breathe. 'Oh, God, swear it again! Swear it again and mean it!'

'Chris,' she moaned, clinging to him, 'he hasn't made love to me! He hasn't!'

The tent flap was swept aside.

The sheikh stood there in the entrance, dark eyes blazing with rage as he saw them together on the cushions.

'Oh!' Bethsheba broke out of Chris's embrace, staring up at the hawk-like face of Suliman, meeting that dark rage and feeling her heart stop violently. 'Suliman, I——'

'I come to offer you supper at my table,' Suliman bit out under his breath, teeth bared. 'Ten minutes! Both of you!' He turned on his heel and strode out of the tent, and Bethsheba's pulses were racing dangerously.

'Does he always speak to you like that?' Chris asked grimly.

She flushed scarlet. 'I told you he hasn't made love to me.'

'Then why are you here?' he demanded. 'Why did you come here?'

Her mouth went dry and she heard herself say hoarsely, 'I didn't come willingly. He kidnapped me!'

'What?'

'He kidnapped me and brought me here against my will. I'm his prisoner, Chris—not his mistress!'

He stared. 'Why didn't you tell me this before?'

She swallowed and said thickly, 'I thought it would be dangerous. This is his land, his *douar*, and these are his men. Suliman is master here, Chris, and we have no option but to bow to his will.'

'Right,' Chris said angrily, 'but I'm master of the helicopter, and as soon as this unwanted supper is over, you and I will be flying straight back to Tangier without passing "Go" or collecting two hundred pounds!'

Bethsheba looked at him and knew suddenly that the getaway back to Tangier, back to the West, back to Chris and everything she had lived with for seven years, was the way back to hell.

The gateway to the West had been slammed shut by the sheikh, and no power on earth would ever prise it open again.

CHAPTER SIX

THEY ate supper at the long arabesque trestle-tables in front of the royal tent. The sun set quickly. It slid behind the sand-dunes like a fire-disc in ten minutes. Camp-fires flickered as darkness fell, and the sky was a theatrical shade of black-red.

Suliman was arrogantly relaxed. He leant back in his chair, head up, watching his people through hooded lids. Food was brought in a selection of brass-domed dishes. It was hot spicy meat in thick sauce, and Bethsheba ate it hungrily, dipping bread in, her appetite as strong as the sheikh's own. Chris was tense, however, and barely touched his food, curling his nose at the taste of the rich sauce.

'Beth!' Chris leant towards her. 'We have to go. It's almost eight o'clock and it takes two hours to get back to Tangier.'

'Yes, of course...' She looked at Suliman immediately, yearning for him, for his world and his ways. Leaving would be so painful. Her eyes traced his strong profile and she longed to kiss him goodbye.

'Sheikh Suliman,' Chris cleared his throat, 'your hospitality has been superb and we both appreciate it. But we must leave and——'

'Of course.' Suliman inclined his head coolly. 'But first we will have dancing.'

'It's very kind of your, sir,' said Chris, 'but——'

'It is our custom,' Suliman said flatly, his tone brooking no argument, and clapped his hands.

At once, music slid into the air. Bells and flutes and skin-drums lilting as the fires blazed and crackled. Khalisha moved out of the shadows, beautiful in a transparent scarlet silk dress that bared her belly, her long black hair flowing like silk as she swayed to the music, cymbals clashing gently in her bird-like fingers.

Even Chris sat up. He was fascinated, captivated, staring as Khalisha danced like Salome for him, twisting and turning in the firelight, her dark eyes never leaving Chris's face, her exotic beauty quite mesmerising.

The cymbal clashed in her fingers as she wound her way to the table, sliding back and forth in front of Chris, her dark eyes as hypnotic as her body was provocative.

Chris's hand shook as he reached for his glass. It was empty. He stared enraptured at Khalisha. Suliman smiled coolly and snapped his fingers. A servant sprang forward, removed Chris's glass and replaced it with another.

'She is magnificent, is she not, Burton?' Suliman drawled coolly.

'Magnificent!' Chris agreed thickly, and picked up his glass, draining it thirstily as he stared, riveted, at Khalisha. His glass was quickly refilled. He drained it again.

The cymbals were clashing furiously. Sweat gleamed on Khalisha's face and body. She twisted and turned as the music rose to its crescendo.

Bethsheba watched, her face white with jealousy, and felt her hatred for Suliman return in waves of dark angry passion. Magnificent! Yes, Khalisha was magnificent tonight—but did Suliman have to say so in front of her?

Suddenly, Khalisha flung herself on the sand before Chris. The music stopped.

'Fantastic!' Chris rose, clapping loudly, and walked across to Khalisha, taking her slender bangled hand as he lifted her to her feet. 'You must come to see me in Tangier! I could make you a star! If you can sing as well as you——'

'Khalisha is of the desert,' the sheikh said flatly. 'She would die within the confines of the West.'

'But she's fantastic,' Chris said, 'the—the best thing...' he paused, frowning '...I—I mean...' He stumbled, shook his head, very pale. 'She's—she's——'

Chris?' Bethsheba stood up, worried.

He stared. 'I—I feel weird...must be the heat and——' He broke off, confused, shook his head again and stumbled.

'Maybe he should lie down!' Bethsheba turned to Suliman anxiously.

Suliman was on his feet, dark eyes contemptuous. 'Maybe he will fall down instead!'

There was a stunned silence.

Chris stared. 'The tea...it was drugged...!' His legs began to buckle and he fell sideways into the table with a crash, sending dishes and cups and glasses crashing everywhere before he landed on the sand with a thud.

'Chris!' Bethsheba ran towards him.

'Leave him!' Suliman's hand caught her, dragged her back. 'My people will attend to him!'

'Let me go, you bastard!' she cried, struggling. 'He might be hurt!'

'You come with me!' Suliman bit out, and dragged her towards the royal tent.

'No!' She stumbled after him, struggling angrily, looking back to see two servants picking Chris up. 'Where are they taking him? What——?'

'To sleep it off,' Suliman said flatly and thrust her into the royal tent. 'When he wakes it will be morning and you and I will be long gone!'

'What...?' Breathless, she stumbled backwards, staring at him, her heart pounding like a drum.

His dark eyes flashed as he towered over her, dominating her in the royal tent with his arrogant regal presence. 'Did you think, *bint*, that I would step back and allow him to take you from me?'

Shaking, she said hoarsely, 'But you promised that——'

'I lied.' He strode to her, his hand biting into her wrist as he pulled her hard against his powerful body. 'But you didn't, did you, Sheba? You told me the truth. That you wanted me, that you hungered for me from the moment our eyes met, just as I hungered for——'

'I didn't know what I was saying!' she protested hoarsely. 'I was trapped! I would have said anything!'

'Well now, *bint*,' he said through his teeth, 'feel the trap closing behind you!'

She caught her breath, staring into that hard face. 'You can't do this...' she whispered. 'You can't just——'

'We leave immediately,' he said flatly, and released her, striding to the table on which lay a collection of clothes. 'Here!' He thrust them into her arms. 'You will dress in these. We will be in disguise, Sheba. And your friend will not find us. Not even if he searches the Sahara for ten days in his helicopter!'

'Chris will scour the desert until he finds me!' she said hoarsely. 'He'll stop at nothing——'

'He will be looking for a sheikh and a golden-haired she-cat!' he drawled softly, dark eyes cynical. 'But he will find only two Bedouin in dark robes . . . and he will pass us by, Sheba. Of that you can be sure.'

He turned on his heel, striding out of the tent. Bethsheba stared after him, her legs weak with fear and her body pulsating with a mixture of anger and excitement.

Staring at the dark red robes in her hands, her mouth shook with anger. How dared he do this? Drug Chris and hold him prisoner while he re-kidnapped her against her will!

The tent flap was swept aside.

'Go away, you bas——!' Bethsheba broke off, her head raised and her eyes glittering with impotent fury as she saw it was Khalisha, and not the sheikh, who stood in the shadowy entrance to the tent.

'My lord has sent me to assist you,' Khalisha said. 'You must dress quickly.'

Bethsheba flung the clothes on the cushions furiously. 'Well, I won't do it!'

'Undress quickly that I may help you,' Khalisha said, moving to pick up the clothes, her dark eyes contemptuous. 'My lord wishes to leave at once.'

Bethsheba looked at her and saw the dislike in her eyes. So Khalisha was still jealous of her relationship with Suliman? Suddenly, hope sprang in Bethsheba as she realised that Khalisha would probably help her escape if she asked her to.

'I—I don't want to go with your lord Suliman,' she said slowly, watching Khalisha.

The girl gave an angry snort. 'Why should any woman refuse a man such as he?'

'But it's true!' Bethsheba said quickly. 'I don't! I want to fly back to Tangier with Chris!'

Khalisha hesitated, then laughed. 'You lie, Englishwoman!' Bending swiftly, she undressed Bethsheba, tugging the gold caftan off her and starting to splash her with warm scented water from head to foot.

'If I wanted to be with Suliman,' Bethsheba said, 'why did I try to escape last night?'

There was a silence. Khalisha looked at her and said slowly, 'Even if what you say is true—what can be done?'

Her heart quickened. Lowering her voice, she said urgently, 'When Chris awakes you can tell him where I am. Tell him how I am dressed and where I am headed. Help him recognise me from the air and——'

'If I did that you would betray me to my lord Suliman!'

'Not if I never saw him again,' she said at once. 'Not if Chris found me and took me back to Tangier.'

Outside, the sound of activity in the camp was growing. Horses were being saddled and the excited babble of Arabic from the men was a sign that the sheikh was leaving almost immediately.

'I will consider it,' *sitt*,' Khalisha said under her breath, 'and we will discuss it no more!'

Relief swamped her. She allowed the girl to finish washing her and dress her in the dark red robes. Her answer had been yes: not in her voice, but in her eyes. She had seen it and known at once that Khalisha would tell Chris where she was when he awoke.

When she was dressed she stood back to survey herself in the mirror.

A desert warrior queen stared back at her. Bethsheba caught her breath. The dark red turban, dark red silk yashmak, and dark red robes of a Hariff of the Auda Khazir lent her an exciting majesty she had never possessed before.

Gold eyes rimmed with kohl appeared out above the dark red yashmak, and she stood with regal dignity and arrogance, the robes lending her character as she put her hands on her slim hips, turned this way and that, her long red oxblood riding boots flashing with gold spurs.

Turning, she strode out of the tent. Her dark red cloak billowed behind her long-legged arrogantly feminine stride. Men flicked curious glances at her, gave deep salaams as she walked past them, every inch a warrior queen.

A tall man was striding towards her in black. A gold *iqal* fastened his black head-dress, and beneath the black robes his arrogantly masculine body signalled to her that it was Suliman, and her body reacted with violent desire at the sight of him.

He stopped in front of her. 'Well, *bint*,' he drawled softly, eyes intent on her, 'you carry your robes as befits a warrior queen!'

She looked at him through her gold lashes and said nothing; her heart was beating too fast to allow her to speak. She wanted him. She hated him. She yearned to both escape and surrender.

'My she-cat,' Suliman said under his breath, and ripped the yashmak away from her face to expose the passionate curve of her mouth. 'My warrior queen!' He dragged her to him without ceremony and kissed her hard on the mouth in front of his men, his arms binding her helplessly to his strength while her mouth opened with a low moan of hatred beneath his, and she allowed his kiss to knock her senseless.

When he drew back his face was flushed and his eyes dark with possessive desire. Bethsheba swayed, consumed with fire and yearning and hatred. How could a man affect her this much?

'Come,' he said thickly, and took her hand, 'we must leave at once.'

Together they strode in dark robes towards the waiting horses. In the flickering firelight the two black stallions were magnificent, their sleek muscles gleaming and water-bottles hanging on their saddles.

'Is Chris all right?' Bethsheba asked resentfully as they reached the horses. 'Did the fall hurt him?'

Suliman's eyes flashed. 'Do not be too concerned about him, Sheba, lest you sting me into the actions of a jealous man!'

'Did you drug the pilot, too?' she asked angrily.

He laughed and drawled wryly, 'The pilot is Auda Khazir, *bint*! We are an ancient tribe—older even than the Berbar. You will find us everywhere——' the white teeth flashed in a smile '—even piloting helicopters in Tangier!'

Suliman mounted his horse, took the reins in strong hands, and sat astride it, magnificent in black robes, the gold *iqal* gleaming in the firelight.

Bethsheba trembled with resentment, watching him for a moment, rebellion in her eyes. Then she tightened her lips with determination and mounted her own horse, lifting her head proudly when she was astride the stallion and meeting Suliman's intense gaze.

'Here.' With a hiss of steel he produced a long curving sword and handed it to her. 'Take this. We face a dangerous wilderness, and you must arm yourself against it.'

'I can't take that,' she said, staring at the scimitar in horror.

'You must,' he said flatly, mouth grim.

'But I thought we were riding to your Great Palace of Suliman and——'

'We are. But it is many hours' ride from here, and we must travel alone to avoid detection.' He held out the scimitar, eyes hard. 'Take it.'

Her eyes met his in tense silence. Slowly, she took the scimitar, and when she realised that her hand was not even trembling she stared at it, at the slender fingers curved around the hilt.

'Sheath it, *bint*,' the sheikh drawled, his black stallion dancing beneath him. 'You have a scabbard at your hip.'

Unsmiling, Bethsheba looked at her hip and saw the black scabbard. Without saying a word, she sheathed the sword, felt it hard against hip and thigh, and then lifted her head to meet his gaze proudly.

'We ride!' Suliman said under his breath, and nudged his horse into a fast canter.

Breathless, afraid and excited, Bethsheba nudged her horse into a canter too and followed him into the darkness, her booted feet thrust into the stirrups and her turbaned head bent to the wind.

They galloped across blackened sand-dunes, neither speaking nor looking to left or right. The thunder of hoofs on the sand, the desert lit with jewelled stars and the receding light of the *douar* all combined to make Bethsheba feel a deep sense of exhilaration.

After an hour they were in the middle of the wilderness, and the empty paradise of sand stretched limitlessly on all sides. Their only companions were the moon and the stars and the wind.

It must have been close to midnight when the temple appeared on the horizon. At first, Bethsheba thought she was imagining it. The vast carved stone walls and the mountainous rocks behind it were just black shapes in the distant darkness. But gradually she realised it was real, and that they were heading towards it.

'Is it the Great Palace of Suliman?' she shouted to him.

'No,' Suliman shouted back. 'But it is our destination tonight!'

The temple rose up in ancient silence as they approached it. The crescent moon and jewelled stars glittering in the dark sky, illuminating the stone walls.

A ruined temple, she realised, staring up in awe. It could have been thousands of years old: the roof ragged with decay, the vast stone entrance scrawled with carvings and words and ornate symbols.

The carvings were magnificent. Her eyes traced them, wishing she knew what they meant, the carved people bowing to carved Gods, and the lettering surrounding the door telling her something she did not understand.

'What is this place?' she asked, haunted by its ancient beauty and the serenity of the silence that surrounded it.

'It is the Temple of Sheba.' Suliman's voice echoed as he led the way, his horse moving with agile grace over the rocks and sand that were the path to the great arched doors.

'Sheba!' She stared at him, her throat tight, and halted the black stallion at once.

Suliman halted too and turned his dark head. 'Do not be afraid of your destiny, Sheba,' he said deeply. 'This is your sanctuary, and here your destiny is strong. In every carving, every wall, every ancient silence lies the truth of your birth. This is your temple, and it is the heart of you.'

He dismounted with masculine grace. His horse swished its black tail, and the harness jingled as it nodded its head. Bethsheba stared at it, then at its master, her mouth quivering with a deep-rooted fear she could not name.

'Were you always going to bring me here, Suliman?' she asked hoarsely.

'Always.' He walked to her, his strong hands went around her waist and he lifted her from her horse to stand before him, pressing her against his hard body as he looked down into her eyes. 'It is written that here shall you understand all. Come... face your destiny!'

They walked up the dark stone steps, and Bethsheba struggled to control the rising tide of nameless fear as she clung to his hand, and walked shakily up those crumbling stone steps. The arched entrance was high and broad, and she stared up at the ceiling, awed by its height.

The corridor they entered was long and high. Carvings flanked the stone walls. At the far end she could see a fierce gold light shimmering with dust.

'This is Sheba's Walk,' Suliman said beside her. 'It leads to the heart of the temple—the heart of Sheba.'

He walked beside her, taller, much taller than she, his head held high, his muscular body cloaked in black robes, the gold *iqal* gleaming on his regal head and his black riding boots echoing on the stone floor, gold spurs jangling as he walked.

Bethsheba had never seen him more magnificent than he was now, and she tried to control her fear, matching his dignity with her own as she walked beside him, her mouth proud, her hand in his.

Suddenly, light blinded her.

'Oh!' Stepping back, a hand shielding her eyes, she cried out.

'Take my hand!' Suliman's dark voice urged. 'Step into the heart with me!'

Blindly, she groped for him. The light was dazzling, but as his strong fingers closed around hers she felt him tug her forward into the light until it hurt unbearably and she cried out, afraid.

Then the light went.

'What happened?' she whispered, rubbing her eyes and peering around the room, eyes dazed. 'The light went so suddenly that I——'

'It is the Tunnel of the Moon,' Suliman told her. 'See—the light pours in through that tunnel in the ceiling.'

Bethsheba lifted her head, gazing up in wonder at the high domed ceiling. A long spherical tunnel sent light pouring in from the silver moon. It landed on a vast gold statue.

Her eyes widened as she stared at the statue, the woman with long golden hair and a split body: the head and torso of a woman, but the lower body of a golden cat with long gold tail.

'Sheba!' Suliman said beside her as she stared at the statue. 'She blinds all who approach with her beauty. Only when you reach her heart are you safe from her light.'

'Her heart...!' Bethsheba looked down to see that they stood on a carved stone heart seven feet wide. 'What does that writing mean?'

'They are the dying words of Sheba,' Suliman told her. 'It means, "I shall return seven times".'

Slowly she looked at the statue, her lips parted.

'Yes, *bint*!' Suliman drawled, watching her eyes. 'You are face to face with your namesake at last!'

'This is her?' she asked, turning to look at his hard face. 'The one you think of when you call me Sheba?'

He laughed softly. 'Did you think it was another woman?'

Hot colour flooded her face. 'I—I wasn't sure...'

'And you were jealous?' He took her shoulders in strong hands and turned her to face him, his eyes blazing with possessive triumph. 'From now on you will show me your jealousy. Your pain. Your rage. From now on, Sheba, you will display your passions—and I will fan the flames or soothe your jealousy at will!'

'Tell me about Sheba,' she demanded huskily, her pulses racing at the thought of what he could do to her if they spent much more time together. 'I want to know about her! Tell me everything! Is she a goddess? A sphinx? A——?'

'This is not Egypt, *bint*!' he drawled. 'We have no sphinx goddesses here. No, Sheba was something quite different.'

'A queen?'

'She was Queen of the Hafu,' he said. 'The Hafu was this area of the Sahara in ancient times. But Sheba was not of royal blood. It is written that she was born of the desert, born in the sands in a goat-hair tent among nomads. That she came out of Arabia in a ship of gold, and that her beauty and courage made her a queen.'

'A romantic story.' Bethsheba smiled. 'But is it true?'

'There is little evidence of her existence, save for this temple and the writings at the Great Palace of Suliman. But I believe in the power of her legend, *bint*. No legend springs from barren earth. I believe she existed, and that she was a warrior Queen of the Hafu.'

'And her seven reincarnations?' she asked, watching him through her gold lashes and feeling her heart respond to the smile that touched his hard mouth as he met her gaze.

'It is written that my ancestor Suliman married Sheba in her third reincarnation in the fourteenth century. She was as beautiful and powerful as her namesake, and she ruled the Hafu with my ancestor Suliman the Great.'

'A fairy-tale ending!' she said, smiling.

'Not quite,' Suliman said flatly. 'Sheba was poisoned by one of her enemies.'

'Poisoned!' She was horrified.

'My ancestor Sheikh Suliman El Khazir built this temple in homage to her beauty and his love for her. He had the words of Sheba inscribed on this stone heart to remind future generations that the Sheba would return.'

'That she would return seven times...' Bethsheba said huskily.

'Yes. And each reincarnation would occur in the lifetime of the seventh generation. Therefore each seventh-generation eldest son is named Suliman.' His eyes glittered. 'And I am he.'

'But I am not Sheba!' she said on an urgent whisper. 'My parents were English! My father a

British army officer! I was born in Bahrain, but——'

'What were the circumstances of your birth?'

'I...' she stared into those dark whirlpool eyes and heard herself say hoarsely '...I was born in a goat-hair tent in the desert on a hot day in——'

'July!'

'Yes!' Her voice was inaudible.

'The seventh!' His voice was deep, urgent, compelling. 'You were born on the seventh of the seventh——'

'It doesn't mean anything!' she said fiercely, her voice a whisper in the echoing stone chamber of Sheba. 'It's just coincidence! My mother was supposed to give birth to me in hospital!' Everything was arranged, but——'

'You cannot arrange fate!'

'No, you don't understand!' she said urgently. 'It was an accident that I was born in the desert! There was an emergency! My father was missing in the desert and my mother——'

'Was called by destiny!'

'No!' she cried again, heart pounding faster. 'She had to go out into the desert, even though she was heavily pregnant. She was so worried—so frantic! She became separated from the men she was with, her pains started, and she stumbled on an encampment where the women helped her and——'

'And you were born,' he said thickly, eyes flaring, 'in the desert! On the seventh day of the seventh month in a goat-hair tent among nomads!'

'Coincidence!' she moaned, clutching his broad shoulders.

'Sheba!' he said thickly, and then his strong hands were pulling her towards him, his hard mouth closing over hers, and as she moaned in breathless excitement so he pulled her closer, and the moon shone down on the statue of Sheba and Sheikh Suliman El Khazir kissed his she-cat until her knees gave way.

CHAPTER SEVEN

LATER, Suliman led Bethsheba out of the temple.

It felt, as they walked through that great stone archway, that it was as it should be, as it would always be, and that she had no choice in what was happening to her.

'We must sleep out here,' Suliman said deeply. 'The temple floor is too hard, and snakes live in the crevices of its walls.'

She controlled a shudder. 'Poisonous snakes?'

He gave a curt nod, moved to his horse and untied the blanket from the saddle. 'We will be safer and more comfortable here in the sand. The shade from the rocks will protect us better than any stone walls.'

Bethsheba went to her own horse and untied the saddle-blanket. It was made of rough thread, coloured in dark blue and red; the royal colours.

'Here.' Suliman walked in his black robes to a niche of sands enclosed by rough stones. 'This will be our bed tonight, Sheba.'

She watched him through her lashes. 'We will sleep together?'

'How else?' he said softly, and a smile curved the hard mouth.

The prospect of actually sleeping in his arms all night sent her pulses rocketing. Lifting her head, she walked to the niche of sands and spread her blanket beside his.

'You may wear your hair loose tonight,' Suliman told her. 'It pleases me. But tomorrow you must hide it. It will be a banner to your friend Burton, and I will not have him see it and stop.'

'I doubt if he'll follow us,' she said with a leap of her heart as she remembered Khalisha. Surely she would tell Chris the truth?

'He will follow us,' Suliman said flatly. 'He has tamed the girl in you, Sheba. He knows I will tame the woman, and he will fight to prevent me from doing so. Come!' He sank down on to the make-shift bed and held out a strong hand. 'Lie beside me, Sheba, and breathe in the scent of your natural home, the desert, and its prince.'

He looked so handsome lying there, one leg bent and black-booted, spurs gleaming from his heels. He rested on one elbow, the black head-dress and gold *iqal* giving him that air of Eastern masculinity that made her quiver with electric response just to look at him.

She lay down beside him, went into his strong arms, and felt a wave of emotion so deep, so strong that she closed her eyes and wondered if she was in love with him.

Suliman relaxed against the blankets, holding her against his chest. His breathing began to even out, his heartbeat slow. The arms that held her felt so right, so natural...

'Suliman,' she asked as sleep crept up on them, 'why would Chris want to stop me becoming a woman?'

'Because he knows he will lose you,' said the deep voice.

'But why should he lose me?' she asked.

'It is your innocence that ties you to him,' he said. 'You are the prisoner of unleashed desire. He will do everything in his power to prevent me from taking you.'

Bethsheba remembered Chris's rage when he thought Suliman had made love to her, and was silent. Was it possible that Suliman spoke the truth? Even she had seen the fury in Chris's eyes, and had known instinctively that it was not the jealousy of a man in love. Then what had it been? Certainly Chris had reacted possessively. But was that possessive rage born of love? No. She knew Chris. He was fond of her, enjoyed her company, and respected her work. But he did not love her.

Nor does Suliman, she thought, and pain tore at her heart.

She had wanted him from the minute she saw him. Wanted him in every way—physically, spiritually, mentally, emotionally: and she had wanted his life too. This life—the desert and the *douar*, the palaces, and the vivid, barbaric luxury of it all.

But why? She had everything she could wish for in the West. Success, money, fame, an exciting career, a lot of friends, and every day filled with appointments and interesting work.

Yet still she yearned for the life Suliman was giving her. For the freedom of the desert, the thrill of walking barefoot, riding bareback, and all with this strong, handsome desert prince at her side, both throwing the confines of civilisation to the wind as they rode across their beloved wilderness together.

Suliman was asleep now; deeply asleep. But Bethsheba was wide awake, and as she raised her head from his chest she sighed, accepting the whirlwind of thought in her troubled mind.

Extricating herself from his arms, she walked softly away from their desert bed. The temple walls rose up before her, but they shimmered, for tears were stinging her eyes, and the carvings wavered like a mirage.

He doesn't love me! she thought fiercely. Why am I crying?

Leaning weakly against the temple walls, she closed her eyes. She was hurt, and she could no longer deny it to herself. The feelings Suliman aroused in her went deeper than physical attraction—but how much deeper? And what precisely were they?

Suddenly she heard an odd sound—a hiss and slither that made her stiffen. Glancing up sharply through a mist of tears she saw Suliman asleep on the rough blankets in the circle of stone.

A long silver snake was undulating towards him.

Bethsheba froze. She tried to cry a warning, but her voice would not work. Moonlight illuminated the snake, beautiful and chilling in its evil as it moved closer to Suliman.

Adrenalin coursed through her body. She was moving silently towards him, her hand instinctively going to her hip. The hiss of steel as she withdrew the scimitar did not wake Suliman as the snake moved into the circle of stones.

It slowly raised its head an inch from Suliman's outstretched arm. The sword flashed in the moonlight as Bethsheba severed the snake's head from its body.

The head flew on to the sand. The body twitched in death-throes and blood spilled out. Suliman woke with a start, staring at Bethsheba as she stood over him in dark red warrior's robes, the bloodstained sword in her hand.

'You saved my life,' he said deeply, and as she looked down into his face she realised she was in love with him.

'It was going to kill you,' she heard her voice say.

Suliman got to his feet. Now it was he who towered over her, handsome in the black robes and timelessly desirable. 'My warrior queen! I was right to bring you here! The temple has brought you face to face with destiny and you can deny it no longer!'

'I didn't even know what I was doing,' she said slowly, wonderingly, staring at his dark, intense eyes. 'I just took the sword from the scabbard and——'

'That is the way of kismet. It comes naturally, without thunderbolts or trumpet calls, as it came to you tonight.' His strong hands touched her waist, drawing her closer as his eyes darkened. 'Sheba! Truly you are she! Our union will be earth-shattering, and our sons will be warriors indeed!'

Her breath caught at the last words and she said, 'Sons!' Her voice was hoarse, her gold eyes wide with incredulity. 'Suliman! What do you mean—our sons will be warriors indeed?'

'What else could come,' he asked deeply, 'from a union between Suliman and Sheba?'

'But it's impossible!' Panic vibrated in her voice. 'You must see that!'

'I see a girl on the threshold of womanhood. And tomorrow night the transformation will be complete when you lie naked and sated in my arms, your innocence a thing of the past.' His head lowered, and as his mouth claimed hers in a deeply arousing kiss Bethsheba moaned, helpless in her fierce desire for him, her mouth opening beneath his and her eyes closing even as she struggled to come to terms with what he had said.

But his kiss was erasing all memory of words from her mind, and when he pulled her down into the bed beside him she gasped as his mouth found her throat and burnt a trail over the throbbing pulse that betrayed her dark passion.

The scent of him was driving her wild as she kissed him back, her mouth on his flesh, his hair, and the scent of Arabia filling her, of horseflesh and leather and everything masculine.

Suddenly he drew back to look at her. He was breathing harshly, his eyes like dark coals. 'You are almost tamed, Sheba.'

'You'll never tame me!' she denied hotly, but he just smiled, his hard mouth curving sardonically as he looked at her flushed face and fevered eyes and knew the truth.

'Come,' he said, turning her to lie against his chest. 'We sleep now. Tomorrow you will enter the Great Palace of Suliman, and after that there is no way back.'

Bethsheba lay with her head on his chest, consumed by emotions and self-doubt. Was he right? Was she almost tamed? But how could that be when she fought so hard to protect her innocence?

Because you're in love with him, a little voice whispered inside her. Angrily, she denied that voice. She refused to think of it! All she felt was physical attraction, and if she ever once allowed that attraction to turn into love she would be lost.

She thought she would never sleep, but of course she did, holding Suliman near as her eyes closed and her breathing slowed . . .

Bethsheba woke from a deeply erotic dream and turned on to her back with a languorous moan. In her mind, Suliman was still making love to her, his hard body moving against hers as she greeted him with wanton eagerness.

'Good morning, *bint*,' Suliman's voice drawled from a short distance away. 'Your dream was satisfying?'

'Oh!' Bethsheba's eyes snapped wide open to stare at him as shame flooded her with guilty colour. 'What—what makes you think I dreamt at all?'

He was standing by his horse and he laughed at her. 'Your soft moans of pleasure, my dove! And the way you slid yourself against me in the night.'

'Oh!' Her flush deepened to burning scarlet. She turned away from him, appalled. Had she really done that? How awful! She could barely meet his eyes.

Suliman watched her in the hot desert stillness. Then he strode slowly towards her, his black robes flickering slightly in the morning breeze.

He knelt beside the circle of stones. 'Do not turn away in shame.'

She couldn't look up, her face burning as his shadow fell over her.

He took her face in one hand and turned her to look at him. 'Sheba,' he said deeply, 'you have the right to feel desire. The right to express it. And the right to incite desire in your mate.'

She closed her eyes to his words, his mouth shaking.

'These are the rights of woman,' Suliman said, 'and it is this deep knowledge of the secrets of your sex that Burton is withholding from you.' He straightened, standing over her, unsmiling. 'Remember that, should you hear his helicopter fly above you today.'

Bethsheba looked up into his hard tanned face in silence, her shame suddenly forgotten. Chris would come. Chris would save her from the destiny that unquestionably awaited her at the Great Palace of Suliman.

'Come,' Suliman said. 'Pick up the blankets. It is time we rode.' He turned on one dark heel and strode over to the waiting horses. Bethsheba watched him for a second, then got up, rewound the red turban to cover her hair, picked up the blankets, and went to her horse.

Suliman watched her with dark intense eyes. When she was ready he gave a harsh cry and nudged his stallion into a fast canter. Together they rode out of the temple and into the hot golden desert, and the sand flew from the horses' hoofs.

What if Chris didn't find them? Galloping alongside Suliman, the wind tearing at her robes, she flicked a sidelong glance at her sheikh. He had said their sons would be warriors. Was he serious? Did he really intend to have sons with her?

When the sun was at its zenith, Suliman indicated they should stop for water and rest. They veered to the left, galloped over a sand-dune, and Bethsheba was astonished to see an oasis ahead.

'How did you know it was here?' she asked as their horses walked to the water, green plants and palms flourishing in the heat.

'I need no city signposts here,' Suliman drawled coolly, 'this is my land and the land of my forefathers.'

She smiled, and dismounted, spurs jangling as she landed neatly on the sand. Suliman dismounted too, and unscrewed his water-bottle, drinking thirstily.

'Drink, Sheba.' Suliman indicated her water-bottle. 'We shall not stop again.'

Bethsheba took the water-bottle from her saddle and unscrewed it. 'How far is the Great Palace?'

'Two hours' ride.'

'So we'll get there in daylight hours?'

Suliman inclined his head and drank thirstily.

Bethsheba watched him through gilt-edged lashes. Suddenly she had to ask, 'Suliman ... when you said we would have sons, were you serious?'

He lowered his water-bottle. 'Of course.'

'I might not want to have sons, though,' she pointed out, keeping her cool.

'A woman who does not want sons?' he queried, one dark brow arching.

''Well—in Western society it happens all the time!''

'Well—in Western society, *bint*,' he drawled sardonically, 'people are brought up to value houses and city streets and jobs. What has this to do with life? With birth and death? With everything that is real and natural? Of course the women choose sometimes to override their instincts. They have been taught to do so.'

'But, Suliman,' she said defensively, 'that's not the point! I don't want to have sons with you! I don't want to go the palace, make love with you, have your sons—or stay in this wretched desert a moment longer!'

'Sheba,' he said deeply, stroking her high cheekbone with one tanned finger, 'you were not born to be kept in dark airless rooms full of recording equipment and money-men. Admit this one truth, and you will be more than meeting me halfway.'

Her face flushed lightly and she said, 'I—I still don't want to have your sons, Suliman! And no power on earth can make me do something I don't want to do!'

'If you truly do not wish it,' Suliman said, 'then it will not come to pass.' He studied her surprised face for a second, then turned. 'Refill your water-bottle. We must ride now.'

She watched him take the reins of his black stallion and mount it, sitting astride it, handsome and clever and strong, his regal profile turned from her, the gold *iqal* on his head-dress gleaming in the sun. He won every argument, no matter how hard she fought, and she wondered for a moment whether she would ever understand him. He had moved heaven and earth to get her by his side, to have her riding with him to the palace of his ancestors. Yet now he appeared to be placing it all in the lap of the gods! He just did that to win the argument, she told herself angrily, and strode to the oasis to replenish her water.

They rode out into the desert together. Refreshed, their horses galloped faster than ever, their sleek black coats glistening. The sun was fierce, and Bethsheba was glad of the protection her turban gave her.

It was an hour later that they heard the helicopter.

Chris! Bethsheba's gold eyes flicked up as she and Suliman galloped across the open desert terrain. The shadows fell over them like a giant black hornet, the sound of the blades scaring the horses.

'Your friend Burton!' Suliman shouted as he rode beside her. 'Let us hope he passes these two nomads by!'

But she knew he would not, and her heart contracted with a worrying mixture of pain and excitement. Chris would take her home! Angrily she pushed the pain aside—what did she care for Suliman? Why should she feel this deep sense of loss?

The helicopter was circling, its engine vibrating, and Suliman's jet-black eyes were narrowed with anger. Suddenly the helicopter started to descend on them, deliberately barring their way.

The horses rose up in frightened protest. Sand flew everywhere, stinging Bethsheba's face and eyes. Her horse veered, as did Suliman's, and they fought for control, their robes billowing as the helicopter landed with a soft thud on the sand.

'Dismount!' Suliman bit out as he saw Bethsheba's horse trying to rear up. 'Dismount!' He leapt off his horse, seeing her fear, and tore the reins from her hands, his black robes billowing as he held hers steady.

Chris was opening the helicopter door as Bethsheba leapt from her horse and fell on Suliman, her hands gripping his strong shoulders for support. Chris's eyes flashed open in angry surprise, but he did not falter, walking towards them in jeans and a white shirt.

'Suliman,' he shouted angrily, 'I'll have you thrown in gaol for this!'

'You are not in London with your money and your lawyers now, Burton!' Suliman shouted back angrily, holding the rearing horses while Bethsheba clung to him and sand whirled around them. 'This is the desert, and here we settle our scores man to man!'

'I can take you to court in Tangier or Marrakech or Rabat!' Chris shouted, blue eyes furious.

'I am a prince of the desert!' Suliman bit out. 'My power and my money are stronger than yours here. If you try to fight me in the cities you will regret it!'

'I'm Christopher Burton!' The helicopter engine was winding down, the blades slowing, the sand settling. 'And this is my star—Bethsheba Lyon! You have no right to take her from me!'

Suliman smiled as the horses began to quieten. 'She came willingly.'

'Then why did you drug me last night?'

'I thought you needed the rest!' he drawled mockingly.

Chris stepped forward, furious. 'Beth is coming back with me.'

'I don't think so,' Suliman said softly.

'Beth!' Chris flung out a hand to her, his eyes vivid blue and angry as he looked at her.

She swallowed on a dry throat, then broke from Suliman and ran to Chris. Her soul was screaming even as she did it, but, feeling unable to do anything else, she flung herself into Chris's arms and buried her face in his neck.

'It's all right,' Chris murmured, holding her, 'you're safe now.'

'Let her go,' Suliman's dark voice said from a short distance away, and she heard a tortured note in it which made her soul cry out in agony even as she fought to be indifferent. 'Let her go, damn you!'

'Go to hell!' Chris bit out, and turned with Bethsheba in his arms to move back to the helicopter.

Suliman moved suddenly, his long-legged strides carrying him to block their path. 'Let her go!' he bit out thickly, barring their way with masculine arrogance, hands on hips, every inch a legend in those black robes.

'Look, it's over!' Chris said tightly. 'She doesn't want you! It was all great fun for a while, but now it's over!'

'Not until she tells me so herself!' Suliman bit out.

Bethsheba couldn't look him in the face. She hung her head, staring at his black leather riding boots, at the spurs glittering gold in the sun, and at the long, muscular legs.

'Beth, for God's sake, tell him!' Chris muttered furiously.

She opened her mouth but no words came out. She wanted to say the words—they burnt in her mind, but inside...inside, her heart was twisting, her soul tearing in two, and as she raised her head to force herself to look at Suliman she met his fierce, passionate black eyes and caught her breath, thinking, I'm in love with him!

'Tell him!' Chris bit out, furious.

She flinched, looked at the sand and said thickly, 'It's over. Leave me alone, Suliman.'

There was a long silence.

'Right.' Chris relaxed, moving forward with her in his arms. 'Now—get out of the way, Suliman and——'

'You do not leave this place with her!' Suliman bit out, barring their way. 'She wants to stay!'

'You just heard her say she didn't!' Chris was absolutely livid. 'I've come hundreds of miles to get her, and I am not leaving without her!'

'Then you will fight for the privilege!' Suliman leapt at him, his strong hand gripping Bethsheba's arms and pulling her away from Chris, ignoring her angry cry as he thrust her aside and moved towards Chris. 'You will fight like a man or go home with your cowardly tail between your legs!'

'Cowardly!' Chris stared at him. 'Now just a minute, you bloody desert——' He leapt at Suliman in a burst of rage and punched him in the jaw.

Suliman's head jerked back. His eyes blazed, his fist shot out, and Chris sprawled back in the sand with a thud, blood on his mouth.

'No!' Bethsheba ran to stop them as Suliman leapt at him. 'Don't fight! I want to go back with Chris! I want to! I want to!'

'Stay back!' Suliman bit out, turning to stare at her.

Chris took advantage of the moment. He seized the hilt of the scimitar at Suliman's hip and pulled it from the scabbard. Standing, he backed away, the sword flashing in his hand.

'Chris...' Bethsheba's blood ran cold as she stared '...put the sword down! There's no need for this...'

'Stay out of this!' Chris flung angrily, and the steel of the scimitar glittered wickedly in the sun. 'She's mine, Suliman!' he shouted. 'I made her what she is, and she made me! I won't let you take her—even if I have to kill you to keep her!'

'No...' Bethsheba whispered, trembling. Chris knew how to use that sword, all right. He was an expert fencer. Every drama school in the world taught its students to fence, and Chris had trained at RADA. He had played Mercutio, Hamlet and every classical role that demanded a perfectly executed sword-fight. Even now he stood in the correct pose: his feet planted firmly on the sand, one turned out, one forward, ready to dance out of the way should Suliman attempt to get near him.

Suddenly Chris flicked the sword in one hand and cut Suliman's black robes open at the shoulder. Suliman sucked in his breath, a hand clamping on his wound as blood ran between his fingers.

'Stop it!' Bethsheba screamed, running forward.

'Get back from him!' Chris moved forward, too, his sword pointing at Suliman's throat. 'Now—get in the helicopter, Beth!'

'But I can't just leave and let you——'

'Get in the bloody chopper!' Chris bit out.

She stared, sweat on her upper lip, her heart hammering in fear. 'He's unarmed, Chris.'

'He wanted to fight, didn't he?' Chris said under his breath, and his sword slid across Suliman's throat, grazing the skin. Suliman didn't even flinch, but his eyes blazed with dark rage.

'I demanded of you that you fight like a man,' Suliman said contemptuously, staring arrogantly down that curved steel blade at Chris, 'not like a bandit!'

'But this is the desert, isn't it?' Chris sneered. 'And there are no rules!'

Anger rose in Bethsheba. Suddenly she found herself unsheathing her own scimitar, and as the steel hissed and flashed in the sun both men turned to look at her.

'No rules, Chris,' she said under her breath, and flung the sword at Suliman. 'No rules!'

Chris stared at her, his face draining of colour.

Suliman caught the sword with one hand, gripping the black handle. He gave a cry of dark triumph, turning on Chris, the blade flashing, and, as Chris danced out of the way, Suliman made an expert thrust, grazing his forearm and drawing blood.

Bethsheba watched in an agony of tension. The clash of steel rang out in the hot desert air. The sheikh was forcing him back, his face tense with primitive rage, and his sword moved faster and faster as Chris retreated, parrying desperately, his eyes wide with shock.

Suddenly, Chris's sword flew out of his hand. With a cry, he stumbled backwards and fell on to the sand. Suliman stood over him, his sword pointing to his throat.

'You are beaten, English!' the sheikh said with dark mockery.

Chris shook with rage but could do nothing to alter his humiliation.

'Don't hurt him!' Bethsheba ran forward. 'Please! He lost his head! He didn't know what he was——'

'I will not hurt him,' Suliman said tightly, 'on one condition.'

'Well?' Chris breathed thickly, hating him, lying helplessly at his feet, the sword at his throat.

'You get back in your helicopter and fly back to Tangier alone,' Suliman said flatly. 'Agree to this and you will go free—unharmed.'

'That's my decision, not his!' Bethsheba protested angrily.

'I hold the sword at his throat, and we have fought for you,' Suliman said harshly. 'He will obey my demand, or pay the penalty!'

'Demand it of me!' Bethsheba said furiously.

'Not here,' Suliman said tightly. 'Not now. You will obey the decision that is made here, *bint*, and come with me to the Great Palace of Suliman!'

'I will not!' she said fiercely, eyes blazing gold.

'Well?' Suliman pressed the sword harder against Chris's open throat. 'What is your decision, English?'

'I want her to come with me!'

'You have fought and lost!' Suliman said bitingly. 'Are you a man of your word—or a snake that crawls on its belly?'

'You bastard!' Chris's mouth shook with fury. 'You know very well I have no choice!'

Suliman's hard mouth twisted in a smile. 'Then go.' He stepped back, the sword at his side.

Chris scrambled to his feet, brushing sand from his clothes, his eyes furious as he moved back to the helicopter.

'Chris, no!' Bethsheba stared to run, panic flaring in her.

'Leave him!' Suliman's voice cracked like a whiplash as his hand shot out to take her arm, yanking her back angrily. 'Do you want to humiliate him beyond endurance?' he demanded, eyes fierce. 'He has fought and lost. Let him go to lick his wounds in private—he will be back, of that you can be sure.'

Bethsheba stood speechless with despair and fear as Chris slammed the helicopter door, his face averted, and the blades were already whirring noisily, sand spinning up as they gathered speed. When the helicopter lifted from the ground and flew above them she hid her face from the sandstorm and thought, I had my chance to escape! I had my chance and let it go!

But he might have killed Suliman! And the sheikh had been unarmed—how could she have stood by and done nothing? She had had to throw that sword and stay with them rather than run to the helicopter and make good her escape.

When the helicopter had disappeared from sight, and the desert was silent again, Suliman drew back to look at her.

'So, Sheba,' his voice was as dark and seductive as his eyes, 'you chose me, after all.'

'I didn't choose you!' she denied hotly. 'I chose justice! I couldn't just stand by and let him wound you seriously—or worse!'

Suliman's hard mouth moved in a smile. 'How you lie to yourself, Sheba.' Suddenly he frowned, and his hand moved to his shoulder, feeling the cut.

At once she looked at the cut, concern in her eyes. 'He hurt you!'

'A scratch,' Suliman said coolly, watching her.

She ignored his male pride and studied the wound with concern. 'It isn't deep, but it must be cleansed.' Quickly she moved to her horse, took the water-bottle, and tore a piece of cloth from her turban, dipping it in water and tenderly bathing Suliman's wound.

'My warrior queen excels as a nurse, also,' Suliman drawled softly, watching her with a wry smile as she attended to his wound.

'All women do,' she said coolly. 'That is their tragedy.'

Suliman laughed under his breath, and said, 'Tonight, Sheba, in the Great Palace of Suliman, you will be taught how a woman really excels—in the arms of a man who desires her above all others!'

Her eyes flicked up in a heart-stopping moment of panic and excitement. 'I should have let him kill you! I should have got on that helicopter and left you!'

'But you did not, Sheba,' he said under his breath, 'and tonight shall you be rewarded in my bed!'

CHAPTER EIGHT

THE Great Palace of Suliman rose out of the desert. Gold-domed turrets and spires pierced the blue sky; ancient bleached stone walls made a sprawl of towers and soaring archways and colonnades. There were thick clusters of Arabic script, gold-meshed windows, ancient drawings embedded in the yellow stone, and everywhere around—all around it, framing it like the golden masterpiece it was—there was sand.

It had about it the look of legend. And of kismet. Bethsheba rode towards it, red robes flying across the black muscled flanks of her horse, and felt moved by the sight of it. Awe-inspiring, it seemed to touch something deep inside her. Love flashed in her eyes and her blood answered the song of Suliman, of his palace and his land.

Dogs scattered as Sheba and Suliman rode through the great stone archway. The horses' hoofs clattered on the cobbled courtyard. Men rushed towards them, men in desert robes, men with deeply tanned faces who called out in Arabic at the sight of them.

Suliman was every inch a prince as he spoke to them in Arabic, the authority in his voice and face quite striking as he dismounted in one dynamic movement.

He strode to Bethsheba, his strong hands encircling her waist, and lifted her down from the horse. The men stared at her, a woman in dark red robes, a scimitar at her hip.

'Well, Sheba,' Suliman said coolly as he looked down his arrogant nose at her, 'do you like the palace of my ancestor?'

'How could anyone fail to be moved by its beauty?' she answered honestly, and lifted her head to meet his gaze with a challenge. 'But I feel sure your ancestor Suliman would not approve of its being turned into a prison.'

'A gilded cage, my fierce dove,' he drawled, dark eyes mocking. 'And, when you are ready to accept the freedom I alone can give, you will be free.'

He turned on his black-leather-booted heel, spurs jangling. His hand took her arm, and he led her beside him across the courtyard and up the ancient stone steps.

The Eastern grandeur of the magnificent hallway they entered took her breath away. Gold-carved walls of marble led up to a ceiling so high that it was almost mist-shrouded, a chandelier of gold oil-lamps hanging mystically from its centre on long gold chains. The floor was marble, spattered black, white and gold, and words were inscribed at the edges.

They walked down a long, echoingly vast corridor. The palace was vast, she realised; how vast, she could not even guess, but as she walked beside her prince she saw fountains and statues in distant walled gardens, arched colonnades and rooms; endless, endless rooms.

As they reached a central square of pillared marble, Suliman clapped his hands twice, sharply.

Doors opened all around them. Women came out to greet him; his women, all ravishing Arab girls with long black hair and eyes of dark fire. Dusky-skinned, nostrils pierced with diamond studs, they were dressed in harem silks of such vivid colour and beauty that Bethsheba felt admiration flood over her at the same time as jealousy.

'Your harem?' she asked through tight lips, turning to look at Suliman, the jealousy laid bare in her fierce eyes.

'They are my women,' Suliman met her gaze, amused, 'but they are not my wives.'

'What's the difference?' Her voice was harsh with jealousy, and she hated herself for being so blatant but she was in the grip of a powerful emotion she had never truly experienced before.

'A great deal, *bint*,' Suliman said coolly, 'but nothing I care to discuss with you in front of them!'

'How very convenient.'

He clapped his hands, gave an order in Arabic, and the women moved towards her.

'Wait!' Bethsheba backed from them instinctively. 'What's going on? Suliman—what did you say to them?'

'I ordered them to take you to a place where you may rest and eat,' he said flatly, face arrogant. 'At sunset you will be brought to me. Until then—recover from your arduous journey and prepare yourself for the night of your awakening.'

'Brought to you!' Her eyes flashed with anger. 'Am I a pomegranate? Or a sweetmeat?'

'Neither has ever been so pampered as you will be tonight, *bint*!' Suliman said, dark eyes intense. 'For at sunset the women will take you to the Great Bath of Sheba,' he said coolly. 'There you will be scented and clothed as befits a queen, in order to meet your true destiny in my arms.'

'In your bed!' she flared hotly, hating him.

'I command it,' he said, lifting his head with absolute self-assurance. 'It shall be so.'

Turning, he strode away in his black robes, leaving her surrounded by the women. Trembling, angry, excited, confused—Bethsheba turned to look at them, meeting their stares with a proud lift to her head.

They took her to a luxurious bedroom scattered with silk cushions and with an air of such slumbrous privacy about it that she felt quite at home. The scent of cassia oil burning in lamps reminded her of Suliman, of the *douar*, of the desert and of seduction.

Exhausted, she collapsed on to the silken cushions. A woman knelt at her feet and pulled off her oxblood riding boots. She flexed her toes and closed her eyes, leaning back among the cushions.

The women moved about her. Someone unravelled her turban.

Suddenly, a gasp and a cry of Arabic made her open her eyes. The women were staring at her, and as she looked at them they dropped, *en masse*, to their knees.

'What's the matter?' Bethsheba quickly looked behind her to see if Suliman had come in, but there was no one there. 'Why are you kneeling?' she asked, then suddenly realised that they were staring at her hair.

Sheba, she thought, touching her hair, and smiled.

So it was true. Everything Suliman had told her about the legendary Sheba was true. The women were treating her as a queen, and she couldn't help comparing their awed worship with the teenage girls who bought her records and copied her hairstyles in the West.

Bethsheba was treated by people in the West as someone very different; very unusual and special. She didn't like it much. It set her apart, quite literally, and made her lonely.

It felt normal, of course, after four years of widespread fame. And the way the women now treated her was no different, she realised, studying their bent heads and the awe in their eyes.

Was this how it was for Suliman, too? she wondered. He was their king. Everywhere he went his people treated him with reverence and respect. He too was set apart; marked out as different.

The women brought her quail eggs, smoked salmon, spiced meat and chunks of bread, a large pot of spicy coffee and a brass tray of sweetmeats. Bethsheba ate hungrily, alone in the beautiful room, closing her eyes as each delicious mouthful filled her.

Sprawling on the cushions, barefoot in her dark red robes, her hair spilling in gold profusion around her head, Bethsheba managed to sleep, quite without design.

She slept deeply, and when she awoke it was because a gentle hand shook her. Looking up into a dusky face with diamond-studded nose, Bethsheba remembered where she was.

It was sunset.

Her body came alive with a sudden leap. Heat and excitement flooded her. She was to be bathed and scented for Suliman. She was trembling as she allowed the woman to help her to her feet. Following her to a small door, she went through it and caught her breath.

Here at last was Sheba.

The bathroom was vast. A circular temple of feminine beauty, it had mosaic floors of blue, gold

and white. The walls shimmered a summer gold;
vast stone pillars gleamed beside the waters. Long
gold-flecked filigree lace hangings covered a colon-
nade at the back, a garden with lush plants and
three fountains.

And there, in the midst of that secret garden,
stood Sheba. The gold statue gleamed, half-cat,
half-woman, and Sheba's legendary eyes seemed to
smile at Bethsheba in the sunset.

The women crowded round her then, and undressed her. At once, Bethsheba lifted her head in
pride, and as the soft-skinned hands stripped her
clothes away, layer after layer of desert nomad's
robes, Bethsheba quivered, reminded forcibly of her
womanhood as she stood naked before them.

The woman knelt to her.

Nude, Bethsheba moved regally past them,
walking to the steps and down into the warm water.
It felt delicious. She slid into it and began to swim,
breathing in the scent of it, rising in soft steam to
the tendrils of her wet hair.

Suliman would be bathing too now, she thought
nervously. Preparing for tonight, when he takes me
in that bed, and her heart hammered violently at
the thought of it.

He will make love to me, she thought; of that
there is no doubt. Her body throbbed with heat
and she floated, golden-skinned and beautiful, in
the warm water, thinking of it, torturing herself
with it, knowing she would eventually cry out with
ecstasy and join him in a greedy, wanton, mindless
purge of all the pent-up desire she had fought since
she first saw him. She hated him for making her
feel this way. Hated him and hated herself. One
lazy hand touched her full breast, felt the nipple
hard beneath her fingers and her heart thudding

harshly beside it. I want him, she thought; I want him and he knows it.

They brought her gown, of transparent gold silk threaded with scarlet. It was exquisitely diaphanous, floating like the wings of a dragonfly. The women dried her with soft towels, scented her with oils, combed her hair with a long golden-toothed comb inlaid with pearls.

When she was dressed a ruby was inserted into her navel and fixed there with paste. They painted her feet with harmel and henna, proclaiming her queen in curling script. Her mouth was painted red; her eyes inlaid with kohl of deepest black.

Finally, a black cloak edged in gold was placed around her shoulders, a black veil placed over her head, and a black silk yashmak drawn over her face. A dazzling gold head-piece was fastened to her hair, making her shimmer in a thousand refractions of light.

Bethsheba was led to the sheikh. Pulses throbbed through her body, making her tremble in anticipation as she walked along corridors, only her kohl-lined eyes visible to those who watched her pass.

The room she entered was not, as she had expected, a bedroom. Frowning, she turned to ask why she was brought here, but the door had already closed behind her.

Suliman stood a distance away, talking to two men. The circular chamber had a high domed ceiling, and light spilled blood-red from its glass into the hushed stone chamber.

'Suliman!' Bethsheba's voice echoed · as she spoke, and he turned, seeing her suddenly, his dark eyes flashing over her with surprise, down to her painted, jewelled feet, and back up to her fierce gold eyes.

He walked towards her in white robes, a gold *iqal* around his head; sheikh once more. On his hand flashed a gold signet ring inlaid with rubies and a crest.

'Sheba,' he said deeply as he reached her, and his hands slid to her shoulders, 'you are more lovely than Scheherazade.'

'What is this place?' she asked, flushing. 'Why are we here?'

'It is the end our journey,' he said deeply, 'and the beginning of all journeys.'

'I don't understand...' She looked at the two men watching them. 'Is this some kind of ceremony?'

'It is our wedding ceremony, Sheba.'

Catching her breath, she just stared at him, her gold eyes wide with shock between the black yashmak and glittering gold head-dress. 'Wedding ceremony?' She stepped back from him.

'Come!' he said urgently. 'Say your vows beside me that we may enter the gateway to paradise.'

'But—but you can't marry me!' she said, appalled. 'And I certainly can't marry you!'

'You must have known this was imminent!' he said flatly, eyes narrowing.

'What?' She could barely get her breath back. 'But you didn't mention it! Not once did you——'

'I said you were to be my warrior queen. What did you think I meant, if not my wife?'

'You said nothing that would indicate marriage! Nothing at all! I would have——'

'You think I intend to have bastards ruling my kingdom when I am dead?' he asked flatly.

Her eyes flared. 'I think you're a fool if you expect me to go ahead with a marriage I don't want!'

'Take care, Sheba!' he bit out, nostrils flaring with sudden anger. 'You insult a prince of royal blood! I am no fool to suggest this marriage! I at least have the courage to follow my desires and my destiny, to fight those who would stand in my way, and demand everything of the woman I want!'

'You want me the same way you want food!' she said fiercely. 'To satisfy a temporary hunger! When you're sated you'll have no further use for me! What will happen then? Will I become one of your women? Bathing the next woman who takes your fancy?'

'Sheba,' he said thickly, hands gripping her upper arms, 'have you understood nothing? You are she I have waited for since birth! You are she with the head of a virgin and the body of a she-cat! You are——'

'That's just a legend!' she protested hoarsely. 'The truth is that I'm just Bethsheba Lyon from London SW3! That I work as a pop singer and don't belong in your world at all!'

'You are the Sheba!' he bit out, eyes blazing. 'And I will marry you!'

'No!'

'You pull back from the gateway because you recognise the scent of death!' he said thickly, holding her tight, though she struggled furiously, fear pulling her apart. 'The death of your old life and all it meant!'

'Of course I pull back!' she said fiercely. 'I can't let you marry me!'

'Yet through the fires of your death will come resurrection! As my Sheba—my destiny and my queen!'

'I'm not Sheba!' she cried, tears stinging her eyes. 'Can't you understand that? You don't want to marry me for myself—only for my resemblance to a dead legend! But I'm not a dead legend! I'm a real woman, made of flesh and blood, and——'

'You're not a woman until you have loved a man!' Suliman said under his breath. 'This one truth, at least, the West teaches its women! Until the moment of surrender you are still a girl, and it is the girl in you who fights for survival!'

'I won't marry you, Suliman!' she broke out hoarsely, recognising his determination suddenly and matching it with a determination of her own as she began her struggle in earnest.

'Do not fight with me publicly,' he bit out under his breath. 'Not in front of my men.'

She looked into his hard, angry face and felt the tears blur her vision. His hands were hurting her. The men were watching, grim-faced. The scent of incense hung heavy in the air.

What choice did she have? Railing against fate in Suliman's palace was pointless. His men were everywhere, and here his word was law. There was nothing she could do, and it was time she faced it.

I can have the marriage annulled later, she told herself fiercely. Or get a divorce. I don't have to stay married to a man who doesn't love me! I don't . . .

Suddenly she was standing beside him, repeating her vows. Her voice echoed around the stone chamber, followed by Suliman's, and a gold rope bound their wrists together for eternity.

When it was over and her shaking hand signed the documents, Bethsheba looked down at her scrawled name and saw she had written, 'Sheba.' She froze where she stood and her heart skipped several beats as she tried to understand how it had happened. It was uncanny. It looked Arabic.

'My queen!' Suliman said beside her, and his hands curled possessively at her waist.

'I don't have to stay married to you, Suliman!' Bethsheba told him hoarsely. 'As soon as I get back to the West I'll file for a divorce, and I'll get one, believe me, when I tell them how you forced me into this marriage.'

'Then I must see to it, my queen, that you never get back to the West!' He released her, clapped his hands together, and the great doors of the stone chamber were flung wide. Three handmaidens stood at the entrance. Suliman spoke in Arabic and the women came forward.

'What now, Suliman?' Bethsheba asked, hating him. 'What new test awaits me?'

'You will find out soon enough, Sheba,' he bit out, and clapped his hands again.

The women took Bethsheba and led her away gently. She was taken down a long corridor, shown to a room, and left inside it, alone, to come to terms with her marriage.

Of course: it was the bedroom.

The great silken bed dominated the room, folds of scarlet silk hanging down beside gold silk, blue and white. Royal blue carpet covered the floor, ornately curved chests were inlaid with pearls and precious stones, and cassia-oil lamps hung around the room.

Bethsheba El Khazir, she thought bitterly, but her heart leapt with pride and excitement too, and—

however hard she struggled not to feel it—the love she felt for Suliman flooded her with such sudden force that she was almost knocked backwards.

How can I love a man like him? she thought furiously, and tears stung her eyes. He cares nothing for me! He uses me, dominates me, kidnaps me and fights me!

Yet she loved him, and the war inside herself raged violently as she tried to reconcile herself to her marriage, and to the moment when he would take her in that silken bed tonight.

Her mouth went dry with pent-up desire as she stared at the bed. Dressed in this erotic Eastern way, painted and scented, she felt like a sacrifice for the sheikh. He only wanted her body. He had made himself clear on that point from the very beginning. He wanted what this night would bring. The satiation of every desire he had ever held towards her.

A door opened on the far side of the room.

Bethsheba gasped, turning.

Suliman entered.

For a second, neither of them spoke or moved. Then Suliman closed the door.

'You are mine,' he said intently. 'At last.'

With a hoarse, angry cry, she flung, 'I will never be yours! No—not even if you brand the name of Suliman El Khazir into my flesh! I will never belong to you—or to any man!'

'You deny me still!' he bit out, making her jump as he came for her, fury in his eyes. 'Even now that we are married! Even now that I have made you my queen—you still refuse me!'

'You force me to,' she said hoarsely, backing away from his anger, 'just as you forced me to ride into the desert with you! Just as you forced me into marriage by——'

'Your memory fails you, *bint*!' he said between his teeth, reaching for her. 'You came to my palace at Agadir of your own free will, and so shall you enter my bed tonight: freely and with excitement!'

'Never!' she flung, shaking.

His hand dragged her towards him. 'From the moment I saw you, I have not been able to think, to eat, to breathe, to live! Not until I had you here in the palace of my forefathers, as my wife, my queen—my lover!'

'Why don't you say what you really want, you coward?' she said bitterly. 'You just want to go to bed with me!'

'Do you think I have had a choice in this?' he asked thickly, holding her still as she struggled. 'Do you think that at any moment, since first I saw you, I have been able to sit down and think about this clearly? It is destiny's hand that has thrown us together, Sheba, and now destiny demands that we release her deepest and most primitive forces!'

'You mean sex, don't you?' she said, her hands curling on his strong shoulders. 'Why don't you say it? Why don't you just fling me on the bed and take me? Get it over with and let me go!'

'You speak of it as an ordeal,' he said thickly, and his eyes were suddenly ablaze with fire, 'and so it will be, *bint*. An ordeal of pain as well as pleasure! You are poised on the brink of woman-hood, and I will take you through the gateway with my body!'

'I can't fight you now, Suliman!' she said rawly, tears in her eyes. 'You are king here, and can do what you will.'

'I am not king without you, Sheba,' he said under his breath, and she was suddenly still, staring at that hard, noble face. 'I am a king only in legend, in the minds of the people for whom the ancient boundaries of Hafu still hold truth. They are as seduced by your legend as they are by mine—just as you were seduced into my arms by the legends of your childhood and the power they still hold for you.'

'Yes,' she said hoarsely, acceptance in her gold eyes, 'it's true! I have been . . . seduced! Seduced by Arabia, by the desert and the memories of my childhood.' Anger flashed in her eyes. 'And you played on those weakness of mine, Suliman!'

'But those weaknesses,' he said thickly, 'are your very essence. They have been buried by the false life you lead in London. But here, with me, you will find truth again. The only real truth—the power of life and of destiny!'

He suddenly ripped the head-dress away, flinging it with a clatter of gold to the floor along with her veil and yashmak.

'Oh!' Bethsheba jerked back in shock as her hair tumbled in fierce gold colour around her slender shoulders.

He ripped the black cloak from her and she was exposed, the diaphanous gold-scarlet gown revealing her full breasts with prominent pink nipples, her slender waist and bare belly, her long slim legs and the gleam of gold between her thighs.

'Ah, yes...' Suliman said thickly, eyes black with desire. 'Yes!'

Heat pulsed through her body. 'No...I don't want——'

'Yes!' he said under his breath, dark eyes flashing up to meet hers. 'Yes, Sheba, you do!' As he stepped closer his strong hands moved to her breasts, and she gasped hotly, staring at him in shock, as his fingers stroked her erect nipples and her legs weakened beneath her.

'Please...' she whispered through dry lips, unable to move away, 'I'm helpless here...I can't get away...'

'You don't want to get away!' he said under his breath, and then his head descended, his hard mouth closing over hers in a kiss that sent the blood pumping through her body.

Her hands fluttered up to his broad shoulders instinctively, weakness invading her like sweet torturous sin, and her mouth was opening beneath his with a moan as she gave in to that kiss, their breath mingling in erotic heat, their tongues meeting, and every light, restless moan from her hot throat betraying her as the kiss deepened.

The strong hands stroked her nipples, inciting hoarse moans of pent-up longing. Her mouth was open and moist beneath his, and as she felt him slowly tug her bodice down she burnt with shameful excitement, loving the feel of his hands on her bare breasts.

When his head bent to take a nipple in his mouth, she almost whispered, 'Yes...yes...!' like a wanton in the grip of blind hunger, and her hands shook as she pushed the white head-dress from him to bare his head to her fingers, thrusting them into his thick black hair and gasping as his teeth bit teasingly into her nipple and pleasure-pain shot like hot needles of madness through her turbulent blood.

He stroked her belly, making her shudder, tension gripping her inside as he touched her, stroked down to her slender hips, and when he heard her moan softly in response he moved his head back to hers, possessed her mouth again with his tongue and deliberately cupped her bare buttocks with strong hands, pushing her slowly against his hardness.

'Oh, God...!' Her voice sounded high and strained as the blood pumped harder and harder around her body. 'Suliman!'

'You are mine!' he said thickly, and then swung her into his arms.

He carried her to the bed and her mind reeled as he lowered her on to its silken folds. He joined her at once, sliding against her, one strong thigh moving between hers to spread her beneath him as his mouth covered hers in a burning, sensational kiss.

He was stripping her slowly, expertly, taking his time, as though taunting her with her own need and forcing her to face it, as his hands pushed the silken bodice off to bare her breasts fully to his gaze, and studying them, straight-faced, without touching them while she shivered in a hot fever of excitement and waited.

As his fingers dropped the silk bodice to the floor her mouth dried, and when those same fingers slowly cupped her breasts like ripe fruit she stared at his mouth and yearned for its heat. As his head slowly lowered she closed her eyes, and when his mouth hovered tormentingly over her aching nipples she burned with intolerable excitement, arching herself towards him until her nipple slid into his mouth.

He closed his eyes with a hard smile and took what she offered him. His strong hands moved down as she moaned softly beneath him, and when they began to stroke her slender thighs she burned with shameful excitement, longing to feel him tug the silken skirt that covered her, longing to feel it glide down softly over her hips, over her thighs, leaving her naked to his gaze and his touch; helpless, burning, yearning.

His mouth possessed hers again, and as the passion rose higher she found herself moving instinctively against him, almost as though she did not know she moved her body, slowly, rhythmically, sensually against the hard thigh that parted hers.

Suliman's strong hands were on her hips, and as his kiss deepened, so one hand moved to slide beneath her, cupping her, pressing her against him, up and then down, slowly, while her soft moans made his control stronger and her resolve weaker.

Touch me, her mind screamed, and she was struggling to breathe, struggling not to scream it hoarsely at him when she felt his fingers loosen the silk skirt at her waist, and she almost sobbed with fierce need as he pushed the skirt slowly, slowly, down over her bare hips, then over her slim thighs.

Her heart was banging like a drum. The silk skirt swished softly on to the floor, and she was naked beneath him, her inner thighs like silk and her blood pulsating to the rhythm of desire.

'Now, oh, queen,' he said thickly, his mouth inches from hers, 'now shall you see your king!'

His hands loosed his own clothing, and she watched with dry-mouthed fear as the white robes fell to the floor one by one and he was bared to her. First his chest, that tanned, muscled, hair-roughened paradise she had longed to explore so many times with her fingers, her tongue, her breath, and as his lower body was bared to her she moaned aloud with sobbing need and terror, her eyes inexorably drawn to the potent throb of his manhood.

He came back to her, nude, and fierce heat burned her as those hair-roughened thighs slid against her silken inner thighs, her hands moving to his chest, her breath coming in ragged gasps.

'I'm frightened...' she whispered thickly as his mouth moved to her throat and he slid closer, closer to her centre. 'Please don't hurt me! Please...'

'The girl must die,' he said, breathing raggedly, 'before the woman can be born. My love...' he began to enter her, his heart banging violently in his chest '...my love...!'

'Oh...!' Her hoarse cry became a gasp of exquisite agony and he stopped, looking down at her, his face taut with excitement as he breathed harshly, fighting for control, and when he pushed again, entered her further, she began to struggle, impaled by him like some pagan sacrifice.

'Move with the pain!' he bit out thickly, and thrust himself inside her to the hilt with a fierce groan of excitement. 'Move with it!'

'I can't!' she screamed in paroxysms of agonised excitement. 'Don't! Don't!'

His mouth tightened; he closed his eyes. Then he gave a low snarl of need and he was moving, filling her, thrusting into her as he made rough sounds of spiralling ecstasy under his breath, and as her screams were ignored so she started to move, anger and pain making her bold as she moved against him, slowly at first, then faster, meeting him thrust for thrust, her eyes staring fiercely at his body as he possessed her utterly.

Then it happened. Like a switch thrown, the pain went and the burning need returned, turning her mindless as their bodies met and clung together, moving like animals, their skin damp with sweat, the sounds they made guttural and wildly exciting.

Love exploded in her like a tidal wave. She was kissing his throat, her fingers pushing through his hair, down his back, over his tense spine and down to clutch shakingly at his buttocks. Suliman's mouth closed over hers with a hoarse groan of answering love, and as he thrust faster and faster so she felt the tension claw at her stomach for release, felt anger and hatred and love mingling together inside her... then her breath was sucked in as though she'd been punched, and her head jerked back, eyes rolling up as she gasped with mindless dark pleasure, the caverns of her mind and body flooding with hot ecstasy as her body jerked up and down like a rag doll, spasms punching the tension from her body.

Suliman's hoarse cries of pleasure were tortuous as he fought wildly to control his own needs, his fingers biting into her as she jerked blindly beneath him.

Suddenly his control snapped. He gave a snarl of dark triumph and slammed into her, face contorting as the first surge of violent ecstasy flooded his body, making him twist against her, his heart thundering and his body shaking. His hoarse cries of pleasure mingled with hers, and as her eyes opened she felt such joy, such excitement to see him thus: out of control and all hers.

As their heartbeats subsided and the waves of pleasure lulled them to rest, Suliman lowered his dark head to her throat, still breathing raggedly, and she felt the sweat damp on his skin. Her arms were around him, tracing the spine beneath her fingertips as they shared the silence. How quickly the pain had been forgotten. Yet how bitter-sweet that pain had been when he'd entered her. She remembered it as though it were fire, and as she did she saw a brief vision of herself as a phoenix, shot down in flames of agony to rise again from the ashes, her wings outspread in triumph as she took the crown of womanhood and changed from a princess to a queen.

Now there was no denial. No more lies to tell herself. Not now, naked and spent in the circle of his arms. She could not stem the flood-tide of emotion and call it fear or anger or physical attraction; it was love.

This is love, she thought; and I'm in it.

'My love,' Suliman nuzzled her throat with his mouth, 'you died like a queen.'

Bethsheba gave a husky laugh, studying him through her lashes. 'Am I a woman now?' she teased. 'No longer a girl?'

'You are all woman,' he said deeply, raising his head, 'as I knew you were when first I saw your face.' He kissed her mouth gently. 'These ripe lips invited me, this lush body tempted me . . . and those sun-ray eyes challenged me.'

'Arabian poetry,' she asked lightly, 'or simple flattery?'

'My lord,' he murmured, a smile on his hard mouth as he looked down at her and added, 'simple flattery—my lord!'

She laughed softly. 'Am I to call you my lord from now on? I don't think I'll be able to, Suliman.'

'Not even here? In the privacy of our bed-chamber?' His eyes glinted with mockery. 'Do you not think it fitting? After all, my love, it is here that I shall master you absolutely. And here that I shall make you do my bidding!'

'As you did just now?' She struggled violently to show her independence, her courage and her own proud arrogance, even though her heart leapt at the thought of more nights like this, more nights when control snapped and she was just a woman, possessed by her man and blind in the grip of her love. 'No man is my master, and I will not do your bidding! I cannot accept it, and I cannot permit it!'

'Can you not, *bint*?' he asked under his breath. 'I am your husband. Your king. You will call me lord voluntarily, or I will make you do so.'

'Make me!' Her eyes flashed.

'Oh, yes,' he said softly, 'it will be so.'

'You can't make me do anything I don't want——'

'Can I not?' The dark eyes mocked her, and as she stared into them she remembered how she had burned to have his mouth on her breast, how she had almost begged him to strip her naked, and how she had clamoured inwardly for him to take her finally, to fill her with his manhood and the power of his body and drive the sweet, tortuous heat to its dark, violent climax.

He could make her call him lord and master. He could make her do anything he wanted her to, and that frightened her, for it showed her how complete was her surrender.

She was desperately in love with him now: and there was no way back.

CHAPTER NINE

THE sound of prayer echoed in the ancient stone courtyard below the bedroom windows. Sighing softly, Bethsheba turned, her warm face nuzzling Suliman's throat. Still half submerged in the deep primal waters of the unconscious, she found herself curving her nude body to his, her mind filled with images of Arabia, of Suliman and of sex.

A hand stroked her tousled hair. 'Are you awake?'

Her gold lashes flickered as she said softly: 'Mmm...'

The hand continued to stroke her hair as the deep voice asked, 'How do you feel this morning, my queen?'

'Marvellous!' she said with a sleepy smile.

He laughed, the sound husky in his throat. 'You are soft and yielding this morning, my love! I think the she-cat is tamed.'

'I'm half asleep,' she said, tensing in his arms, afraid he might have guessed her real feelings for him. 'Of course I'm soft and yielding!'

'Do not stiffen with pride, my love,' he said deeply. 'I want to see you like this. A woman has many sides to her—I want to see every side of you that exists.'

'You've seen so many,' she said, forcing herself to relax again, loving the feel of those arms around her and the feel of his nude body against hers. It was as though they had been lovers forever.

'I wish to see many more,' Suliman said. 'You are seductress, warrior, she-cat, sated lover——'

'And sleepy woman?' she teased huskily, nuzzling his throat.

'Soon, perhaps,' he said deeply, 'we will see the mother in you.'

She tensed, staring at his throat. 'The mother?'

One strong hand moved to her belly. 'You may have conceived last night. You may conceive to-night. Soon I may have the son I have yearned for, and——'

'Conceived!' She had forgotten all about that! In her blind passion she had welcomed Suliman's hoarse cries of release last night without considering the fact that his seed was shooting irreversibly into her womb with each shuddering gasp. 'I didn't think of it! I didn't think!'

'Does the thought of bearing me a son fill you with such dread?'

'You know it does!' She felt such a fool! How could she have forgotten?

'Yet you welcomed my body with the passion of a woman wailing for her demon lover.' The strong hand cupped her chin, forced her to look at him. 'What will you tell yourself if you have conceived? That I forced it upon you? That you were an innocent party in the conception?'

'You know very well that I had no choice in what happened last night!' she said, her cheeks burning with hot colour. 'I admit, I did...I...I did enjoy it. But that doesn't mean I——'

'Do not lie to yourself, Sheba.' The dark eyes seemed to probe her soul. 'You are a woman now, and as such must accept that your mind knows exactly what it is doing: always.'

'But you didn't ask if I wanted a son!' she said fiercely, her face burning now with resentment and embarrassment at his words. 'You just thrust the decision upon me with no way out! It wasn't what I wanted! It wasn't what——'

'I think you have conceived!' Suliman cut in in a fierce whisper, his eyes intent as he stared at her flushed, frightened face. 'You have!'

'Don't be ridiculous!' she denied in a hoarse rush. 'How can you possibly even——?'

'You are a woman, Sheba, and it is your womb that will carry my son. How can you not know what is in your own womb? How can you not know the dark, primitive truths of your own body?'

She stared at him, struck dumb with fear. He was just trying to frighten her.

His hands covered her belly. 'Your anger and fear stem from your knowledge of conception. Never before have you shown such a hysterical reaction!'

'You're mad!' she whispered, hating him violently as she suddenly pulled out of his arms. 'Mad!'

'Hysteria means womb,' Suliman said coolly, watching her. 'Did you not know that?'

Fury rose in her overwhelmingly as she sat up, eyes flashing. 'If you think I'm going to stay here, trapped in this intolerable situation with a raving lunatic for a moment longer than I have to, you're out of your mind! I wouldn't give you sons if you went down on your bended——'

'We are man and wife now,' he cut in, eyes hardening. 'You will stay here as my queen and conduct yourself as your new status demands.'

'And provide you with a ready-made dynasty? Go to hell! What about my life? What about my career?'

'The career you longed to escape!' His eyes spat contempt. 'Do not try my patience, Sheba! The life you led in the West was stifling you—killing the life force daily! That is why you ran to me when I called, and that is why you will stay.'

'You forced me into a marriage I didn't want!' she cried bitterly. 'You forced me to sacrifice my innocence beneath your insatiable demands! Now you would force a son on me that I——'

'I did not force anything!' he bit out, sitting up, eyes leaping with rage. 'Nothing I have done has been against your will, and until you admit that to yourself and to me we will have no peace!'

'I don't want peace!' she said furiously, hating him as she faced him across that silken bed, both of them naked and burning with a whirlwind of dark emotion. 'I want to go home! I want to go back to Tangier and to the West!'

'The West is closed to you forever!' he snarled. 'Why must you turn your face from the truth?'

Rage exploded in her and she hurled herself at him, screaming senselessly, hitting out blindly, her hands beating at his chest and his shoulders, her nails trying to scratch his face as he fought her back, finally managing to catch her flailing arms, his fingers biting into her wrists as the air was fraught with bitter sounds of violent emotion from them both.

He was breathing harshly as he took control of her. 'You fight yourself, not me! Your own desires, your own needs, and your own secret wish to remain here with me!'

'You'll twist anything to your own advantage,' she choked out, heart thundering as she accepted defeat bitterly, her hands clamped by his like manacles on her wrists, 'but it won't change the way I feel! I hate you and I want to leave!'

'My love,' he said thickly, eyes fierce, nostrils flaring, 'you only hurt yourself.'

'Don't call me your love!' she flung bitterly, tears stinging her eyes. 'You don't give a damn about me! I'm just a possession to you!'

'Possession,' he said quickly, 'is nine-tenths of the law!'

'But it has nothing, nothing and *nothing* to do with love!' she said rawly, and the tears threatened to engulf her, overwhelm her, choking her so violently that she felt her chest welling up with them, pain stinging her heart, her soul, her mouth, nose and eyes.

Suliman watched her in tense silence for a moment. Then, 'Love is the plaything of Western vanity. It has nothing to do with life or with the succession of a throne. You are not here to be loved, *bint*, but to be a queen.'

'Oh, God, you bastard!' she said hoarsely, fighting, with every ounce of pride left her, not to cry. 'How can you sentence me to a loveless life of duty!'

'Because it is written,' he said tightly, mouth hard.

'It is not written!' Frustration made her voice choked with emotion. 'It's just a dusty old legend, and one I will not agree to play out with you. Do you call this freedom, Suliman? Is this the wonderful "freedom" you spoke of when we first——?'

'We will not discuss this here,' he bit out, and thrust her from him, getting out of bed, his nude body magnificent as sunlight touched its tanned, muscled, hair-roughened splendour.

'When will we discuss it, then?' Bethsheba demanded hoarsely, hating him as she sank back on her heels, watching him from the bed and feeling more frustrated and alone than ever in her life before.

'This afternoon,' Suliman said under his breath, and turned to look at her, dark eyes hostile. 'I will send for you and we will talk.'

'And in the meantime,' she asked bitterly, 'what am I to do? Sit in your harem and bathe myself all day?'

'No, *bint*,' he said bitingly, nostrils flaring, 'you will bathe and dress immediately! Then you will be taken to the House of the Artist in the Seventh Courtyard!'

'The House of the Artist?' she demanded angrily. 'What are you talking about now? What artist?'

'You will find out, *bint*,' he said tightly, bitterness in the hard line of his mouth as he snatched up a dark red caftan from a chair and pulled it over his head. 'Until our appointment this afternoon, Sheba—I bid you good day!'

'Wait!' she cried in consternation as he strode to the door and pulled it open. 'For God's sake, Suliman! You can't just walk out like this! Not in the middle of an argument as important as——'

'I see you alter your tone, *bint*,' Suliman said bitingly, turning at the door with hostile eyes, 'but only when I alter mine! If you wish it to be this way between us, carry on! But it will be a marriage-bed of scorpions, and, believe me—I will sting you to death before I allow you to sting me!'

The door slammed behind him so violently that the sound was like a slap in the face to Bethsheba, who flinched, staring at the closed door with tears burning her eyes.

He didn't love her! He only wanted her to bear his sons and be a constant living replica of a gold statue that his people worshipped! It was intolerable!

She threw herself down on the pillows, sobbing uncontrollably. What a monstrous tangle she was in. Did he really think her pregnant? It didn't bear thinking about. How could she possibly be pregnant...after only one night of lovemaking? She wouldn't let herself be! She wouldn't have it, wouldn't let it...

Sitting up, she took deep breaths, fighting for calm. Of course she wasn't pregnant. It was just Suliman's nonsense making her hysterical, frightening her out of her wits. If she was pregnant all hope of getting out of this without serious trouble would be finished: she would have to have the child, regardless of where she had it or who eventually looked after it.

But I'm not pregnant, she told herself. I'm not pregnant and I'm not Sheba and I'm not staying here a moment longer than I have to.

The women came to her within minutes of Suliman's leaving. They took her to bathe in the presence of Sheba, and as she floated in the warm water she looked at her gold-skinned body and saw the marks of Suliman's passion, dark and excitingly vivid on her flesh. Pride warred with anger, and passion tipped the balance as she looked down at those marks and shuddered with remembered excitement, closing her eyes, the steam rising to dampen her face and hair and make her remember... Oh, he had been so exciting, so masterful, so expert and so passionate!

The House of the Artist was quite a long walk.

The Great Palace of Suliman, she realised, was almost a city in itself. There were acres of corridors and colonnades, more gardens with statues and fountains than she could count. One circular pillared courtyard had a gold-domed roof and doors leading off it: doors with the sound of offices within which the sound of typewriters and fax machines and telephones made her stare in shock as the women urged her to follow them.

Suddenly they were out in a vast sprawling courtyard. It was filled with noise and people and life. There were stalls of food, of ripe oranges and sticky dates and fat olives. The scent of fresh meat and fresh-baked bread filled her nostrils as she walked.

People were everywhere, with dark faces and chattering voices. She passed a kissaria filled with a profusion of scents: jasmine and oleander, marigold and musk. There was a silk shop, and the array of wild colours made her stop, delighted as she fingered the fuchsia-pink and firecracker-red, the aquamarine and sunset-orange.

A coffee-shop made her burst out laughing, staring at the ancient stone building with its jaunty Arabian sign. Chairs and tables sat outside it, brilliant white in the sun, and people sat there lazily, drinking spicy coffee and eating Turkish delight.

Then they were walking down a long, cool stone alleyway. It had high crumbling walls, and Bethsheba's dress rustled as she walked, her white silk head-dress and white yashmak hiding her golden hair and skin from the people.

The Seventh Courtyard was utterly charming. With ancient yellowing walls and tiny huddled houses, it had a lovely square with trees and plants, a circular fountain, and an ambience of artistic bohemia.

The House of the Artist itself was a tumbledown building of yellow stone. A beaded curtain hung over the entrance, a dog sleeping in the hot sun outside it and the scent of coffee wafting from within.

Bethsheba was urged inside.

'Hello!' she called, and her voice echoed.

Her gold-sandalled feet click-clacked on the stone hallway, the cool air instantly reaching her as she heard, with some surprise, the hiss of air-conditioning.

Walking through the first stone doorway, she entered a large airy room. Paintings and statues were stacked higgledy-piggledy everywhere. Some were unfinished, some complete. An easel stood by the window, sun shining on bright wet oil colours on the canvas.

The style was recognisable. Edouard de Chanderay, she thought, staring in amazement. Whoever had done these paintings and statues was imitating de Chanderay with considerable skill.

A footfall behind her made her turn.

'Hello.' A tall man with a red-gold beard and straggly hair stood in the doorway wiping a knife dry on a cloth. 'You must be Sheba.'

'Yes!' Her eyes raced over him, recognition shocking her into silence.

'I'm Edouard de Chanderay,' he said, extending a clay-caked hand. *'Enchanté, Madame El Khazir!'*

Silent, awestruck, she took his hand and shook it, still staring up at that familiar face, the fierce blue eyes brilliant amid that red-gold hair: a lion's mane was so fitting for the face of a genius. He was one of the most respected artists of the time, and she felt herself deeply honoured to even look upon his face.

'Forgive me,' she said huskily when she saw his quizzical frown, 'I'm staring, I know. But—but I can't believe you're here! It doesn't seem real! How did you come to live in this place? Don't tell me the sheikh kidnapped you too!'

Chanderay laughed drily. 'No, of course not!' The light French accent was pleasing to the ear, softening his every word with a trace of summer and sophistication. 'I came of my own free will— and with the greatest of pleasure, I can assure you.'

'But how?' Bethsheba was still incredulous. 'I mean—how did you find this place?'

'I flew to Marrakech and turned right,' drawled Chanderay, white teeth flashing against that red-gold beard. '*On y va!* I have coffee with halva in the kitchen. I will tell you my story there—before we start our work.'

She followed him along a winding corridor and found herself in a small sunlit kitchen, the ancient stone painted thick white and hung with jaunty mugs and photographs and wicker plant-baskets. There was a photograph of Chanderay with Picasso, and Bethsheba looked at it with a sense of wonder.

'I've been here five years already,' Chanderay told her as he poured rich coffee into two cups, and set halva out on a brass plate. 'And I can't tell you what a difference it has made to my life.'

'The privacy?'

'*Alors!*' He laughed, blue eyes flashing to her face. 'No reporters! No crowds! No fans! And above all—no phonies standing around discussing my paintings in order to impress their friends!'

Bethsheba took the coffee he handed her, and smiled at the French painting and lettering on it:

'Chaperon Rouge cherche jeune loup'—Red Riding Hood seeks young wolf!

'Here,' Chanderay perched on a white stool, 'nobody cares about my reputation. They just admire my status, my paintings—and then they get on with their own lives! There is no invasion of privacy. I am accepted for who I am—not for the proclamations of the Western Press.'

'You found all that a headache?' She nodded, understanding. 'Yes, it can be distracting at best—painful at worst.'

'Besides,' Chanderay shrugged broad wiry shoulders, 'all this colour and life in Suliman's world! What a fabulous place it is! The weather, the noise, the landscape, the flowers...'

'It's paradise, isn't it?' she agreed, and her gold eyes slid to the window of yellowing stone behind him, half in sunlight, half black shade. 'But how did you find it, Chanderay? It's hardly a major place on the tourist trail.'

'I met Suliman in Paris,' he said simply.

'Paris!' She stared, eyes wide.

'Yes, he's a very cultured man, isn't he? Deeply artistic, highly educated, very progressive in his attitudes.'

Bethsheba just stared, speechless. Were they discussing the same man? Sheikh Suliman El Khazir, the man who had re-introduced her to the wilderness of the desert, the barbaric luxury of Arabia, and the freedom of everything that went with it? Of course, she had grown so accustomed to his perfect English—with only a light Arabic accent that grew stronger when he was angry—that it had never occurred to her to wonder where he had acquired it.

'Suliman came to an exhibition of mine,' Chanderay told her. 'We hit it off instantly. He loved my paintings and sculptures—he bought several of them on the spot. We ended up talking for hours, and finally met for dinner at Fouquet's on the *Champs Élysées*. I spent the evening complaining—as usual!—about the lack of privacy my success had brought me. I complained about the Press, about modern life, about phonies and about my growing inability to believe as strongly in my work because of it as I once had.'

'You lived in Paris at the time?'

'I had an apartment in Paris—a villa in the south: Grasse, to be specific,' he said. 'Suliman suggested a month's holiday at his place in the Sahara. I was going to Marrakech that summer anyway, so it seemed quite predestined. I took him up on it.'

The mention of destiny took her breath away. Quickly, she said, 'You came here? To this palace? Not his House of the Seven Suns at Agadir?'

'I came straight here,' he agreed. 'Stayed for a month, fell in love with the place, and couldn't bear to leave. I went home, sold my villa and came straight back with as many things as I could carry!' He laughed. 'I've been here ever since.'

'You rode from Marrakech?' she asked, frowning. 'By horse? That must have been a terrible journey!'

'Rode!' He burst out laughing. 'Of course I didn't ride! I flew here in Suliman's private jet!'

'His jet?'

'Yes.' Chanderay's straggly red brows lifted. 'Didn't you know Suliman had a jet? There's a landing strip at the back of this palace. Haven't you seen it?'

Bethsheba stared, shaking her head, her eyes wide with shock as she reeled under the impact of all this information from a renowned genius who obviously knew Suliman El Khazir better than she did.

Chanderay idly handed her a sweetmeat and took one for himself. 'Yes, it's really very handy. I can fly anywhere I want, come back when I like, live with one foot in the West and one in the East.'

'You continue to go back, then,' she asked shakily, struggling to accept all of this, 'to the West?'

'Of course! I am not a complete lunatic, *madame*! The art world is in the West, and I need it as much now as I ever did. The peace and anonymity I need is here, in the East. But I need to exhibit my work. I need to sell it and I need to keep my name in the public eye. These things are important to every artist, no matter how successful he becomes. An audience, after all, is still an audience, and I do not paint solely for my own pleasure. Like small boys, all artists need to cry, "Look, look what I have done!"'

Bethsheba laughed, fellow-feeling in her gold eyes as they met his. 'It's no different for little girls!'

'Of course.' Chanderay smiled, inclining his head. 'For you, it is the silence when you hold a perfect note and let it fly above the music, knowing that those who listen are as impressed by it as you.'

She flushed a little, lowering her lashes at the accuracy of his statement. 'I still find it incredible, though,' she said huskily, and looked up at him, 'to think that Suliman brought you here...'

'Yes.' Chanderay nodded. 'I am proud to be his friend.'

She smiled, touched.

'And you must be very proud,' he added, 'to be his wife.'

A shiver ran through her as her heart skipped several beats. Chanderay thought Suliman loved her. The pain suddenly returned, and with it the sting of rejection as she remembered what Suliman had said this morning: love is a plaything of Western vanity and has nothing to do with the duty of a queen.

He would never love her. Never; and suddenly the pain was intolerable.

'Shall we get on with our work?' Chanderay drained his coffee and stood up.

'Our work?' She looked at him with a jolt.

'Didn't Suliman tell you?' He frowned with some surprise. 'I am to sculpt you.'

'Sculpt me!' Bethsheba stood up, staring in awed disbelief. 'You! Edouard de Chanderay!'

His frown deepened. 'I am flattered by your awe, Sheba. But I would rather not encounter it here. This is my sanctuary. Here, I am just a man who paints: I would prefer to keep it that way.'

She flushed. 'I'm sorry...forgive me...'

'Ça fais rien.' He shrugged. 'You must have the same pressures, the same violation of privacy. All I ask is that you remember why I came here, and treat me as the man you find me—I have the right to be real while I am still alive.' A smile touched his mouth and his blue eyes glittered. 'Time enough to be a genius when I am dead!'

Bethsheba laughed, and followed him out into the hall, then up the winding white-painted steps to his studio which overlooked the bohemia he had found here, the huddled yellowing houses and acres of blue sky so clear that it seemed closer to God and eternity than any sky on earth.

'Remove the yashmak, please,' Chanderay said as they entered the studio, 'and the cloak and veil. Suliman wants your statue to do your beauty justice.'

The veil, cloak and yashmak fell to the floor, and Bethsheba posed on the white stone plinth in white harem silks, her breasts full and straining at the white-gold bodice, her belly left bare, her slender legs clearly visible beneath the white silk skirt. Bells on her ankles and gold hair tumbling down around her slender shoulders, she posed like a legged mermaid, her hands lifting strands of hair behind her head, her spine arched like a bow. The statue would be unutterably sensual.

'Tell me of your work,' Chanderay asked as he made a primary impression of wet clay, his strong fingers kneading it into shape. 'Your career must have introduced you to many fascinating people.'

'It has,' she said, smiling with pride as she watched him, 'but I think the most incredible thing about it has been meeting such famous people and finding they have heard of me!' She laughed, lifting her brows. 'It never ceases to amaze me!'

He nodded. 'And that will never change. One meets people one admires and is astonished to find admiration in their eyes, too.' He slid a finger over her clay shoulder, rounding it deftly. 'You will be happy here with Suliman. He understands artists, and his love for you can only grow.'

She stiffened, pain in her eyes. 'I might not be happy here. Certainly not if I'm being turned into a statue of an old dead legend!'

'You're used to fame,' he said, frowning at the obvious emotion in her voice. 'Surely this is no different?'

'It feels different!'

'I don't see why.' He said, 'It was inevitable that Suliman would marry an artist.'

She stared, lips parted in surprise.

'Now—could you resume the pose? Yes...arch your back...flaunt your sensuality for the man who has commissioned this statue!' His eyes danced. 'You are Sheba—remember?'

For hours they worked in the sunlit studio. Chanderay's hands and fingers moulded the clay lovingly. A pot of water beside him had knives, spatulas and needles it in which he used, wetting the clay constantly with a small soft-haired brush. The scent of the clay was in her nostrils as she sat in her provocatively sensual pose by the stone window, but the clay itself was all over Chanderay's hands and bench and clothes.

At three o'clock, Suliman sent for her.

With a thudding heart, Bethsheba slipped her cloak, veil and yashmak on and left Chanderay's house, preparing herself to see her new husband and hear the answers to the questions she had asked this morning.

The two handmaidens had an armed guard with them, and Bethsheba walked in the centre, escorted as befitted a queen—or a prisoner. Back through the teeming alleyways and courtyards she went until the royal quarters loomed ahead in yellowing stone, and as her eyes traced the gold carvings on the walls she felt a lift of her heart and thought: home.

To her surprise, she was led to the office section in the circular courtyard that was the entrance to the royal palace. The handmaidens led her across the marble floor, typewriters and fax machines clattering louder now as she approached a large oak door.

Inside the room, she stopped dead, catching her breath. It was a modern office, with a champagne carpet, mahogany desk, black leather chairman's seat behind the power-desk, a fax machine in the corner, and vast panoramic windows at the back.

Outside, on a long strip of black tarmac in the desert, glittered a bright red Cessna private jet. The jet gleamed at her, symbolising everything that was Suliman, as it stood, a brilliant piece of twentieth-century power, on the stark landscape of the desert.

Her image of Suliman collided with the reality and split apart into two men, deeply opposed, the schism healed by her presence and by the deep split in herself, which she was only now beginning to understand as she stood in that modern office in the barbaric palace and stared out at that jet.

The door closed behind her. Bethsheba whirled, heart in her mouth.

Suliman closed the door slowly and leant on it.

CHAPTER TEN

SULIMAN wore an expensively tailored grey suit that fitted his broad shoulders to perfection, a dark red silk tie gleaming against impeccable white shirt and a tight grey formal waistcoat, a gold watch-chain glittering across it.

He was more handsome, more sexy, more formidable than any man had ever been to Bethsheba, and in the darkness of his eyes lay the desert barbarian who had kidnapped her on horseback, dragged her into life, and taken her, last night, to an ultimate surrender that had changed her forever.

'Suliman,' she said huskily, and her love for him shone with dark gravity from her eyes as a lump formed in her throat.

'Well?' His voice was as hard as his mouth as he spoke. 'What runs through your mind, *bint*?'

She tensed, saying, 'I can't believe it's taken you so long to reveal this side of yourself!'

'Why?' he asked tightly. 'Do you prefer it so much to the desert sheikh you first met?'

'No . . . you don't understand. I——'

'I understand only too well!' he cut in with a harsh laugh, and gestured with one strong hand to the window. 'You come here and see my Cessna on the tarmac and suddenly realise you can——'

'Chanderay told me you had a jet!' she broke in urgently. 'I already knew before I got here.'

'Chanderay.' He nodded, eyes hostile as they flickered over her. 'You liked him?'

157

'Very much. Suliman, I can't believe you have him living here!'

'No,' he drawled tightly, 'a respected artist living here, in the home of a desert sheikh! Quite inconceivable!'

'Suliman, I didn't say——'

'Of course not,' he said with a harsh laugh, and pushed away from the door, striding round to his desk with masculine arrogance, sitting in the black leather chair, every inch the chairman of the board with his dark head back and his dangerous eyes focused on her with dark hostility. 'Sit, *bint*. We have so much to talk about!'

Bethsheba moved to the chair opposite him, sank down on it and faced him across the desk, aware of the exciting role-reversal: he in Western power clothes, she in seductive Eastern silks.

'Chanderay told me how you met in Paris,' she said carefully, 'at an art exhibition.'

'You are so impressed by my Western inclinations,' Suliman said with a dangerous look in his eyes.

'I feel we will have more to share now,' she said.

'Yet this morning I was a barbarian holding you prisoner,' he said tightly. 'Well, well, well. How quickly things change.' He shut the lid on a box of cigars which had lain open, and watched her, rapping long fingers on one arm of the black leather chair.

'This morning you shouted at me and slammed out of the bedroom for no good reason!' Bethsheba reminded him tensely.

'You threatened to end our marriage, *bint*,' he said flatly, eyes narrowing. 'What did you expect me to do? Smile and put you on a plane back to Tangier?'

'I didn't know you had a plane!'

'But you do now,' he said coolly, one hand gesturing to the view behind him, 'do you not?'

Bethsheba was silent, studying him as the pain returned, spreading deep into her soul, as she looked into that hard face and knew her love would never be returned. Never.

'So,' Suliman said softly, 'now you see me differently. I am no longer the barbarian you rejected so often, but a civilised man with a lot of money, power and, above all, a private jet.'

Colour flooded her face. 'You're twisting my reaction!' she said angrily. 'You must see that it makes a difference to our relationship—to our marriage and future!'

He smiled, eyes hard. 'A marriage you previously detested.'

'Because I thought we couldn't possibly hope to make anything of it!' she lied in despair—how could she tell the truth? That she had been in love with him for days? That none of this made any difference to her feelings for him—if anything it only deepened her existing love to a well-spring she had never believed she could feel.

'You did not want this marriage,' Suliman said, his arrogant head back as he regarded her contemptuously through heavy-lidded eyes. 'You were afraid I could not hold my own in Western society. How could you marry such a man? How indeed? Only a fool marries for love!' His eyes flashed as he drawled with a sneer, 'Now you find I can more than hold my own in your society—you suddenly find our marriage not only acceptable but desirable!' He gave a cold laugh, his face hard. 'If you were not so beautiful I would despise you!'

'You should have told me sooner!' Bethsheba said angrily, stung by his contemptuous remarks. 'You shouldn't have kept the truth about yourself secret from me!'

'Why?' he asked flatly. 'Would you have gone to bed with me sooner if I had?'

Her breath caught at the insult. 'My God, you bastard...'

'Would you?' He got to his feet, dark brows rising. 'Or shall we find out? Hmm?' He walked lazily around the desk, but there was nothing lazy about his eyes or his mouth; both were hard and hostile and deadly with intent. 'Take off your cloak,' he said, standing in front of her and thrusting his hands in his pockets. 'Come on. Take it off.'

Bethsheba watched him with eyes that hated him. 'Go to hell!'

He laughed, and his hand gripped her arm, lifting her ruthlessly to stand before him. 'Take off your cloak, Sheba,' he said coldly, 'that I might better see what my Cessna jet has bought me!'

Her mouth shook with anger. 'I'd rather die than ever let you see me or touch me again!'

'Yet you longed for pleasurable lovemaking from your desert sheikh!' he drawled tightly. 'And last night—you got it! You had to go through a pointless marriage ceremony to get it—but everything has a price, does it not, *bint*? And perhaps one night of pleasure was all you ever wanted from me.'

Bethsheba whitened. 'I don't want anything from you!' she said hoarsely, and turned on her heel to walk out.

His hand caught her wrist and jerked her back against him. 'You wanted me!' he bit out thickly. 'You wanted sex from your desert sheikh and you got it! But now you find yourself married and a prisoner for life! What better time to make friends with your gaoler than when you see his private jet parked outside and realise he is a very rich gaoler!'

'You didn't ask me to marry you,' she said fiercely, 'you just bombarded me into it!'

'And how you protested!' he bit out. 'Until you were in my bed!'

'Shut up, you——'

'And once you had had your pleasure you started talking of home again! Of London and Christopher Burton and your career!'

'I feel awful about leaving him like this!'

'But you feel no compunction about leaving me!' he shouted hoarsely, eyes blazing, nostrils flaring, magnificent in his rage. 'You would leave me without a second thought!'

'They're relying on me!' she whispered, unable to tell the truth, to tell him she had to leave because she had committed the ultimate folly of falling in love with him. 'It's not just my career—hundreds of other people are wrapped up in it, and I'm the central pivot! How can I just walk out and——?'

'Liar!' he bit out, eyes hating her. 'You want to go back! Now that you have had your little...' his lips curled with contempt '...desert adventure! You want to go back and test your hard-won experience on other men! On the Western men who would be so much more acceptable to you!'

She broke away from him, gold eyes flaring with rage. 'You don't love me, Suliman!' she accused shakingly. 'You don't love me and you never could! You only want me because I look like Sheba! But I'm not Sheba! I'm myself!' Tears stung her eyes

and she whispered hoarsely, 'Myself; I'm myself!'
She repeated, 'Myself, Suliman!'

'And you only want me when I am the sheikh of
your primitive fantasies!' he bit out thickly. 'You
want me to make barbaric love to you, then dis-
appear into the night as fantasies so conveniently
do! As the sheikh, you rejected me—rejected my
world, our marriage, and everything I offered you!'
His eyes burnt her with contempt. 'Now that you
see my jet and my power and my Western clothes
you find me more acceptable!'

'You dressed me up as an Arabian queen before
you married me!' Bethsheba shouted angrily. 'You
didn't find me very "acceptable" as myself!'

'You do not behave like an Arabian queen,' he
bit out, 'and it is time you were disrobed!' One
hand ripped the yashmak and veil from her, flinging
them to the floor.

'Oh!' She backed, gold hair tumbling around her
shoulders. 'You—barbarian!'

Rage turned his eyes black. 'Barbarian?' he
shouted. 'I will give you the barbarian you want
so badly!' And his hands tore the cloak from her,
ignoring her angry cry.

'I don't want the barbarian in you!' she
screamed, hatred welling up in her as she backed
in the diaphanous white-gold gown. 'I don't want
anything more to do with you ever again!'

'Do you not, *bint*?' he bit out thickly, and one
hand shot around her waist, pressing her wriggling
body against his. 'Shall we put that to the test?'

'No, don't . . . !' She sucked her breath in as his
other hand touched her breast, bare and ripe beneath the white silk bodice.

'Yes!' he said under his breath, stroking her
nipple to erect obedience, his eyes ruthless as he

saw her quivering response and the hot flush that stained her cheeks. 'You want it badly!' His hand angrily tugged the bodice aside, baring her to his gaze. 'And you will admit it, Sheba—or find yourself raped on the desk of my Western power!'

'Stop it!' she shouted hoarsely, but he was pushing her against the desk, his eyes murderous, and those strong thighs were parting hers as he cupped her buttocks and lifted her on to the desk. 'Don't...' her whispered plea was despairing '...please!'

His head swooped, that hot mouth taking her nipple, and Bethsheba gave a hoarse moan of pleasure, her hands thrusting into his thick black hair and her body arching towards him as images of what he wanted to do to her flickered through his mind vividly, and she knew the thought of being raped on the desk by him was intolerably exciting.

His mouth lifted, covered hers, and as her lips opened with a moan of fierce pleasure beneath his her blood pulsated through her body and she was gasping as his strong hands yanked the bodice right down, trapping her arms at her sides with the sleeves and baring her to the waist, a helpless captive as his strong hands felt the taut hardness of her nipples and the fierce bang of her heart.

'You want me!' he said harshly, his breathing ragged and his face darkly flushed. 'You would like me to take you—now; here on this desk without ceremony!'

Consumed with molten desire, she whispered fiercely, 'Yes...yes!'

'Then prove it, Sheba!' he said hoarsely. 'Press yourself against me and beg me to do it!'

Moaning, her voice whispered, 'Take me...take me...' and her hands stroked his neck as she kissed him fiercely, running her fingers through his dark hair, arching her body against him and feeling the sharp needles of excitement burn her as her erect nipples rubbed against the expensive material of his waistcoat.

She lifted her hand and pressed it to her breast, arching again as she offered herself to him, and he bent his head and took her nipple, her moans of need growing as the emotions that blazed inside her began to coil to tension again and she knew the release would blast them out of her system, knew that Suliman's lovemaking would force those violent emotions from her body as he took command of her again.

'Take me!' she whispered fiercely, blood pulsating like wildfire through her body. 'Take me!'

Suliman was breathing harshly, his face flushed dark as he pushed the white silk skirt up over her hips, and when she begged him again to take her, he slowly eased the white silk briefs down over Bethsheba's thighs, watching her with dark anger as she began feverishly to unbutton his expensive Western suit.

'I will be clothed, *bint*!' he bit out thickly, hands hurting her wrists as he stopped her undressing him. 'I am the master, and you the whore!'

Rage flashed in primitive desire through her and she tried to hit him, saying fiercely, 'You bastard!'

His hands went to the grey trousers, unzipping them as he spreadeagled her, and pushed them hard down over his hips, 'Bastard or no, you still want me!' he said hoarsely, and the hard jut of his manhood against her softness made her cry out in harsh, fierce pleasure as he entered her and found her more than willing. 'Oh, yes...!' he said thickly, inhaling sharply, gripping her buttocks, his eyes blazing. 'Yes!'

He impaled her with one thrust, and her guttural cry of pleasure matched his own as he held her tight against him, his face contorting as he began to thrust into her, the desk slamming with each movement, the lamp falling to the floor and shattering, unnoticed.

They clung to each other, hatred and rage and desire blending into one as they made love like enemies, their bodies unleashing violent passion as the harsh cries they made were issued against sweat-damp skin, their mouths colliding in a ferocious kiss of intolerable emotion.

The excitement was so fast and violent that she could not hold out against it.

Bethsheba jerked in mind-blowing release, dark pleasure flooding the caverns of her mind and body as she gasped and writhed against him, her eyes rolling up into the back of her head and her heart banging out of control.

Suliman was snarling as he thrust harder and harder until he snapped into a harsh cry of agonised pleasure, and then he too was lost in the ferocious violence of his release.

It felt as though every emotion in them both was being channelled between them in a vast current of energy, blazing between their bodies in those precious moments, like an electric storm flaring up to almost kill them as they jerked and writhed their way to peace.

But it was not peace that filled Bethsheba when at last Suliman rested his head on her shoulder. It was pain. Oceans of pain, flooding her as she held him, her body damp and throbbing with a sense of loss as she felt that sweat-damp head on her bare shoulder, felt the flickering of his wet lashes against her throat.

He pulled away without looking at her, as she had known he would, and the tears that stung her eyes were blinked back in fierce pride as he turned from her, adjusting his clothing with a grim expression and running a hand through his dark hair when he was once again the man of power, his clothes as immaculate as they had been when he had first arrived.

Silence filled the room. Bethsheba tugged her bodice back up and her skirt down: shame was too easy an emotion to deal with when contrasted with the pain.

'My plane will take you to Tangier in the morning.' Suliman's voice was without emotion. He stood with his back to her. There seemed nothing more to say.

Bethsheba slid shakily off the desk, retrieved the rest of her clothes and moved to the door, her face white with pride. Slipping out into the corridor, she felt the hot tears slide over her lashes, felt her mouth tremble, and walked quickly to the nearest sanctuary: the courtyard close by with its plants and flowers and fountain.

Like a dam bursting, the tears came, and she sank blindly on to the ancient wall beside the fountain, burying her face in her hands.

Later, in her private quarters, Bethsheba sat on the windowsill, red-eyed, and watched the sun set. It had a golden glow about it tonight; a fiery disc sinking behind the yellowing walls of the palace and turning them shimmering gold.

How could she leave Suliman and all he had given her? Meeting him had been like being reborn.

Meeting him had been like meeting her mirror image. Her other half. The male side of her that would never be given physical life.

Bethsheba was a child of two nations: kissed by the sun of Arabia, tempered by a formal education in England, strengthened by the bitter fight for survival after her parents' death and, finally, polished by Chris Burton into the acclaimed singer-superstar she was now.

Yet the desert called her: those first, vital years were not to be denied. The secret longings of her childhood in Arabia had exploded from the moment she had met Suliman, and she felt alive for the first time in her life.

Tears pricked her eyes. Sighing heavily, she let them fall. Her eyes were swollen with weeping. She hiccupped softly every now and then, a hand at her red eyes like a sad child's.

'Suliman . . .' she whispered.

A knock at the door made her jump. Not Suliman! She couldn't let him see her like this! He didn't know she loved him, and he must never know—never! Terrified, she wiped the tears from her eyes and struggled to appear composed.

'Come in!'

A handmaiden entered, gave a deep bow, and approached with a note in one slender hand.

'Thank you,' Bethsheba said thickly, accepting the note and staring at it. The handmaiden hovered, smiling. Bethsheba had to open the note in front of her, though her stomach felt as though she were going down too fast in a lift.

Of course, it was from Suliman. 'Dine with me tonight. We will discuss divorce proceedings.'

So cold, curt, clinical. It hurt to look at it and to see how utterly detached he was from the whole thing. Icy and precise like a surgeon cutting out a cancer.

How unlike the man she had come to know. The man with the dark, dangerously intense eyes who had kidnapped her, flung her head first into excitement, adventure and wild, heady desire.

Suliman.

Tears stung her eyes. She wished the damned handmaiden would leave her! Her hand crumpled the cold, cutting note and she thought, I hate him! How could he do this to me?

The argument with him still rang in her ears. How the hatred had poured out of him! Biting out angry remarks, insulting her deliberately, mocking her every word, and, finally, taking her with hot rough anger across his desk.

Oh, she had begged him to do it and begged willingly. The thought of the hard, sexy body encased in that formal suit had made the hair on the back of her neck stand on end with excitement.

But she had also known they had to be earthed: both of them. The emotion flying around in that room had been like a pressure cooker, and the ultimate explosion like megawatts of electricity suddenly released in a flash of power between them as they'd climaxed in violent paroxysms of ecstasy.

The note was still in her hand. She looked down at it.

Suddenly her lashes flickered and she was still.

Slowly, she smoothed out the note.

Was this really from Suliman? This icy and emotionless note? Even if he hated the sight of her he would show more than this. This note was so icy that it wasn't even businesslike.

It was as though he was hurt.

'Oh . . .!' Inhaling sharply, Bethsheba stood up. He couldn't be hurt! It wasn't possible! Suliman? Hurt? But he didn't love her! He had only wanted to bed her! She meant nothing to him! Nothing at all . . .

'But what if he's hiding it?' she said aloud. 'I've been hiding it for days! Why shouldn't he?'

She broke off, suddenly meeting the concerned gaze of the handmaiden. There was a brief silence. The woman thought she was mad, obviously, and Bethsheba almost agreed with her.

The handmaiden motioned for Bethsheba to follow her. Judging from the sky, it must be bath-time, she guessed, and her heart leapt at the prospect.

Now she had a chance! She would see Suliman tonight for dinner—it wasn't much, but it was better than nothing, and maybe she could even win him over if she tried hard enough.

The scented bathroom gave her time to think. Naked, she floated in the warm water, turning this way and that, staring at water-lilies beside her and the gold-domed ceiling above.

Suliman must feel something for her. His emotional outburst this afternoon proved that. He had been enraged, furious, his passion more dark and violent than ever before.

But how could she tell him she loved him? Her heart ached and she closed her eyes, despairing. Her pride was at stake! Love was a no-pride situation sometimes, but in this case the knife-edge of rejection was so dangerous that she could not risk it.

No, there had be be another way. A way to say 'I love you'. A way to say it without risking total humiliation and rejection. But how? How could she do it?

Suddenly she saw Sheba.

Gold-almond eyes watched her serenely from a ravishing gold metal face of high cheekbones and full, pouting mouth, her hair long strands of pure gold coiling around nude shoulders and bare breasts.

That's it! That's how I'll win him over!

Bethsheba swam to the far end of the bath, climbed up marble steps and went to the private gardens to stare at the statue. She couldn't go dressed as a cat, but she could wear those ruby scimitar earrings and the ruby necklace around her lovely throat.

Suddenly she turned, motioning the women to come to her. They clustered around her, staring at the statue as she indicated what she wanted, and the laughter that echoed around the courtyard was wonderful, for it made Bethsheba feel, at last, a real part of life here.

They had such fun together that evening, laughing as they dressed her as Sheba. The earrings were brought to her, and the necklace, and one of the women rushed off to find the right dress for Bethsheba to wear with it to please her royal husband.

The gown was breathtaking. A gold-belled skirt and gold silk bodice made her gleam from head to foot like that statue come to life. Kohl lined her beautiful gold-almond eyes, and the rubies at her ears and throat flashed blood-red warrior colours as she moved.

Suliman awaited her in the great banqueting hall.

Heart thudding, Bethsheba walked in her open red sandals, bells jangling softly against bare thighs and ankles as she moved. If this didn't work, nothing would. She had to persuade him she loved him, and that the Eastern side of his personality was what she loved most of all: not the Western.

Suliman stood at the far end of the arabesque hall.

He stood with his back to her, but even thus she could see the proud arrogant nobility of the man she loved. The black evening suit he wore had Savile Row stamped all over it. He was magnificent, his wealth and power an aura around him; a passionate man tempered by the majesty of his character.

He turned and saw her.

Lifting her head proudly, Bethsheba met his powerful stare with courage, and as his eyes raced over her she was Sheba; for one brief moment his destiny stared him in the face.

The recognition flashed between them. Then it was gone as Suliman hardened his heart to her, and the icy tones of his voice almost cut her as he said, 'Everything is arranged for your departure. You will fly to Tangier at 09.00 hours tomorrow.'

'Oh . . . !' The disappointment was a sledge-hammer in her stomach. 'I—I see.'

'It is quite safe. My pilot is well-trained; the jet checked thoroughly before each take-off.'

Struggling not to show the hurt that raged in her, she said thickly, 'Thank you. I—don't know what to say.'

'Say nothing.' His mouth was as hard as his eyes. 'You will be gone from here and we shall never meet again. No words are necessary.'

She nodded. Speech was impossible.

'We must discuss the divorce arrangements.' Suliman thrust his hands into the pockets of the black evening suit. 'It can be arranged discreetly. No one need know. I will have the papers sent to you. You will sign and return them. It could all be resolved in a matter of weeks if you co-operate.'

Again she nodded. Her face was white and she was shaking. Was her skin always this cold?

'If there is a child from the union...' Suliman began to say, but broke off, glancing away, his mouth tightening.

The emotion in his voice made her stare, breathless with hope. Surely he couldn't be as distressed by this as she? The silence lengthened. She could be still no longer.

'Yes?' she asked huskily, staring at the hard averted face. 'If—if there is a child?'

He looked at her suddenly, his eyes hard, and bit out, 'You come to me as Sheba! Why?'

Her courage vanished. 'I felt like it.'

Fury blazed out of the dark eyes. 'A whim? A little diversion? An amusement?'

'N-no,' she stammered, grabbing her courage by the scruff of the neck and dragging it back, 'because I thought it would be fitting.'

'Fitting?' he ground out, eyes dangerous. 'Fitting to taunt me with what I cannot have! Sheba, you push me to the very limits of my self-control! The sooner you leave this palace and my life—the better!'

He turned on his heel, striding angrily away from her. He was walking out! She couldn't let him go! Not with that black emotion in his eyes—a blackness that could be pain!

'Wait!' she cried hoarsely, running after him. 'Wait, Suliman—don't go like this! Not when I——!'

'You want my self-control to break again, do you?' he bit out violently, turning on her, eyes blazing. 'As it broke this afternoon? You want me to destroy what little dignity we both have left.' His mouth shook. 'I am your king!' He breathed harshly. 'Do not push me to another display of barbaric fury!'

'That's not what I want!' she said urgently, her courage growing. 'I only want to talk. That's all. I want you to stay and dine with me, as arranged— so we can talk.'

'The time for talk is over!' he said thickly. 'Everything has been said! You wish to end our marriage and leave this place. Very well—all arrangements are being made. But do not ask for talk, Sheba, for I have nothing to say to you!'

He wrenched open the door.

'No!' she cried hoarsely, and gripped his arm with possessive fingers. 'No... you can't end it like this! Not like this, Suliman...please!'

'It ends as it ends!' he said under his breath. 'And I cannot stand to see you like this!' His eyes burned over her suddenly, his voice roughening as he said thickly, 'Sheba incarnate. My destiny, my queen, my love. Your body is more beautiful than it has ever appeared to me. Your face...' His eyes flicked up, saw the shock in hers, and flashed with fury, his mouth tightening to a white line as he bit out, 'Go back to the West! Go back to your gaoler! Go back to everything that is false! I was wrong to bring you here!'

'No, Suliman,' she whispered hoarsely, 'you were right to bring me!'

'I was wrong and I have paid the price!' he bit out. 'I thought you wanted me. I thought you wanted everything I could give you, but I was a fool!' His eyes blazed and he said thickly, 'And now it is over. Goodbye, Sheba. May the West bring you everything you dream of, for I know now you will not find it here.'

He left the room, slamming the door behind him.

Bethsheba stood, shaking and dazed, staring at the closed door as tears stung her eyes and threatened to spill out over her lashes. His words were spinning in her mind, turning blindly as she sifted the pride and arrogance and hatred to find love.

He could love me, she thought, trembling with passion. He could, and I must not let him go.

CHAPTER ELEVEN

'SULIMAN!' Bethsheba cried, wrenching open the door. 'Suliman!'

He was turning the corner, and his footsteps echoed alongside her passionate cry, but he did not turn. Bethsheba almost crumbled, leaning against the wall, her hot face cool on the stone as she fought for strength.

If he did not love her she would humiliate herself. But if he did—if there was a chance, just a chance that he was as much in love with her as she was with him, then she had to fight for him.

But what if he only wants Sheba? she thought, tears burning her eyes. A golden statue to keep prisoner at his palace? How could she bear a life like that? With a man she loved?

And if she went back to the West? Her heart sank like a stone at the prospect. Oh, the loneliness of that life! The grim recording hours, the airlessness and lovelessness, and the endless hard grind of touring in buses and hotels and fast food on the road.

Here, with Suliman, she would have the love she so badly needed. Here she would have the love of a king, a king she loved desperately. She would have a baby to nurture, a kingdom to rule over, a desert to be free in, horses to ride ... and a jet to fly her back to the West whenever she wanted to go.

Bethsheba ran along the corridor. Where had he gone? She was breathless, her eyes searching frantically for Suliman, but he was nowhere to be seen, and her fear made her weak as she began to doubt that violent emotion in his voice and the black pain in his eyes.

He was a proud man, though. A king. A warrior. He would never show weakness by telling her of his feelings—not unless he was completely sure of hers.

And how could he be sure of her feelings? She had kept them hidden! At every turn of events, every moment she had spent with him, her will had been concentrated so hard on appearing nonchalant.

So if Suliman cared anything for her—of course he would hide it! His pride would demand it, and Sheikh Suliman El Khazir was nothing if not a proud and noble ruler.

That only left one option—she would have to tell him.

Determination strengthened her. She resolved to open every door until she found Suliman, even if it took her all night in this damned great city of a palace.

She opened doors. Her red sandals click-clacked as she ran from kitchens, to bedrooms, to dining-rooms. There were women's quarters scented with musk and oleander. There were rooms of cushions and music and idle chatter.

Suddenly she pushed open a door and saw Suliman.

In the open doorway, she stared at him, and he looked up from where he sat in the dark leather chair, his hands filled with papers from a white silk box.

He stood up angrily and the box crashed to the floor.

Out spilled the photographs, the Press clippings, Bethsheba's face and name emblazoned on headlines from a thousand different magazines and newspapers.

Slowly, she raised her stunned eyes to his face.

'Get out!' Suliman bit out through white lips. 'Get out! Do you think I want you here?'

'I'm in love with you!' Bethsheba whispered hoarsely.

The silence was thick with emotion. Suliman was rigid with pride and disbelief, the Press clippings scattered at his feet and anger blazing in his dark eyes as his last and greatest secret was exposed.

'I'm in love with you!' Bethsheba said again. 'I don't care why you took me or how it happened or when I fell...I only know I'm in love with you, and that I can't leave.'

'Get out!' he said thickly, and turned his back on her.

She winced, staring, unable to reply.

'Why do you just stand there?' Suliman bit out under his breath. 'Does it please you to know how completely I am yours? To know I have been in love with you from the very beginning?'

'Suliman——'

'You have seen my Press clippings of you! You have seen my love and my obsession!' His eyes blazed. 'Now you have your triumph, Bethsheba! But I do not have to tolerate your presence for a second longer!' He lifted his head arrogantly. 'Go! Go on—get out!'

'I can't go,' she said shakily. 'I love you!'

'Ha! This morning you called me a barbarian and demanded your freedom! Now you love me!'

'This morning I believed you were indifferent to me!'

'This morning you did not know I had a jet!'

Bethsheba's eyes blazed fierce gold. 'You lied to me about yourself!'

'I omitted to tell you,' he bit out. 'That's not the same thing.'

'It is to me!' Her mouth quivered. 'I felt as though you only wanted my body! Do you know how that feels to a woman? I'll tell you—it feels painful! It feels isolating! It feels horribly, horribly lonely!'

The dark lashes flickered on his hard cheekbones. 'How could you think that? You knew I was prepared to fight armies in order to bring you here!'

'But I didn't know that at all, Suliman!' She took a step towards him. 'I didn't. I—I felt so hurt. I felt so frightened for the future. Particularly this morning when you were so cruel. And last night when you said love was the plaything of Western vanity.'

'What did you expect me to say?' he demanded tightly. 'That I was hopelessly in love with you?'

Her breath caught and she reached out a hand. 'Suliman...!'

'No!' he said thickly, angry suspicion in his eyes. 'Do not reach for me now! If love truly existed in your heart, you would have shown it this morning—after I had made love to you.'

'But I was afraid to!' she protested hoarsely. 'I woke up married to a man I barely knew. A man who repeatedly told me he only wanted sex from me. A man who had hidden half his true nature from me, leaving me with only guesswork and fear to go on.'

He stared, his face tense. Then he looked away, mouth hardening, and muttered roughly, 'How can I believe you? It seems so improbable!'

'Yet it is when something is most improbable that it becomes a real possibility,' she said urgently, watching his face. 'The likelihood of someone's being right increases with the amount of people trying to prove him wrong.'

Suliman gave a hard smile. 'You are persuasive, Sheba, but——'

'It's improbable that you've followed my career for so long,' she pointed out huskily, heart thumping. 'Improbable that we should have shared so much without my realising you knew who I was all along.'

The dark eyes flicked to hers. 'I could not let you see. It would have destroyed the beauty of our shared world.'

'I understand that, my darling!' she said as tears stung her eyes. 'And I'm glad I found out now— at the last minute.'

'Why?' he asked sharply. 'Because it makes you feel——?'

'It makes me feel our marriage could really work,' she said quickly, 'just as finding out about the Western side of your nature makes me believe our marriage was ... meant to be.'

His head came up sharply to stare at her.

'Now I know,' she said, 'that you could share my world with as much love as I now share yours.'

He stiffened, his face hard. 'How do I know you really mean that?'

'Suliman, trust your instincts.'

He watched her, dark eyes intense.

'Did you know I was in Tangier?' Bethsheba asked. 'Was this planned from the very beginning?'

'No.' He shook his dark head. 'But I recognised you as I rode up that day. I recognised you and—

and saw the excitement in your eyes as you saw me.'

She flushed, smiling. 'And that was the moment you decided to kidnap me?'

'No.' His black lashes flickered. 'It was later. When you came to sing for me.'

Bethsheba smiled and in the silence he studied her. Then he started to walk towards her. Her heart skipped with hope, but she stayed where she was, not daring to move until he told her he loved her. Oh, please let him love me, she thought wildly. Please let him love me—we're so close now...so close to true love.

'I fed you honeyed bees and fantasies,' Suliman said softly, watching her face, 'fantasies I suspected you shared. And you glowed with excitement, my love! You came alive under the sway of temptation! I could see the love of the desert in your eyes—the love of adventure and excitement and freedom!'

'I wanted this so much!' she said hoarsely. 'I couldn't believe I was actually face to face with a real sheikh!'

'So,' he said under his breath, 'you fell for my image too?'

Her mouth went dry. She had to be truthful. 'At first...yes! You looked so sexy in your desert robes, Suliman!'

He laughed softly, and one hand cupped her face. 'And you wanted me to abduct you? To take you on horseback to my *douar* and make passionate love to you?'

'Yes!'

'You wanted me to take you back to the childhood you have never been able to forget!'

Her heart almost burst with emotion. 'Suliman, I love you!' she said hoarsely.

'My darling!' he murmured, and swept her into his arms, holding her close, pressing her face against his dark throat. 'I've loved you forever! From the moment I saw your face, to this moment of revelation!'

'Oh, Suliman!' Her arms were around his neck, holding him close enough to drown in the familiar masculine scent of him. 'Would you really have let me go? Would you really have put me on that plane!'

'With the greatest reluctance, my love,' he said thickly, crushing her to him, 'but yes—I would have done it!'

She closed her eyes, overwhelmed by how nearly she had lost him.

'I couldn't have kept you here against your will,' he said deeply, 'however desperate I felt not to lose you. It would have been inhuman of me...monstrous...an affront to liberty.'

'Yet you felt no such compunction when you first kidnapped me,' she said huskily, 'and I'm glad!'

'I knew as soon as I had you here—my bride, my love, my lover—as soon as you knew the truth about my life and my love for you...' he drew back to study her with lazy, arrogant charm '...I knew you could not fail to love me!'

She laughed in delight at his arrogance. 'Did you indeed?'

He laughed too. 'I knew you would love me. I knew it.' The smile faded from his dark eyes. 'But that is why I lost control this afternoon. That is why I made love to you so brutally on the desk. The pain went so deep, Sheba. And the sense of loss was overwhelming. I—could not accept what was happening. That I had brought you here, made you my queen, made love to you under terrible pressures of self-control. Watching your arousal, feeling it, being a part of it—I was on the brink of ecstasy all the time, yet fighting not to lose control until you had. And then...' his eyes darkened '...then you rejected me. You rejected me and everything I had given you. I could barely stop myself tearing the bedroom down around your ears with cries of rage and——'

'Don't!' she whispered, holding his strong shoulders. 'Don't remind me of my own terrible pain this morning.'

He studied her in silence for a moment, then said deeply, 'I never guessed for an instant that your rejection of me hid such love.' His hand stroked the blonde hair back from her face. 'I have never loved a woman as I love you. You are everything I am myself—except in a woman.'

'And you are everything I am myself—except in a man,' she said with a smile lighting her eyes.

'My warrior queen!' he said under his breath, and then his mouth claimed hers in a kiss that made her moan with delight, her fingers shaking as they pushed into his thick black hair, her mouth opening beneath his passionately as their bodies swayed.

When he dragged his mouth from hers many moments later, she struggled to breathe, her heart thumping like mad as she met those passionate dark eyes with answering hunger.

'I will see you queen beside me!' Suliman said roughly. 'I will see my son grow and ripen in your belly! I will see you in ecstasy in my bed for the rest of my life!'

'Suliman, I love you!' she said hoarsely, and pressed her mouth against his in a kiss that made him emit a rough sound of passion under his breath before kissing the life out of her.

'How soon can you send for your things?' he asked thickly as he drew back. 'I want you in residence with me wherever I go. If anything of yours needs to be brought here——'

'I don't know!' she said huskily. 'I must contact Chris, though, and let him know I'm safe. That's an important——'

'Do not worry,' Suliman said deeply, 'we will fly to Tangier together tomorrow, tell him of our marriage and see what he is prepared to accept in settlement of your contract.'

She studied him, uncertain. 'Settlement of my contract?'

'Unless you wish to continue with it,' Suliman said, dark brows lifting.

'You mean—you'd accept that if I wanted to?'

'But of course!' he said at once. 'I do not wish to strangle your creativity! You are an artist, and will always need that outlet. I merely suggested settlement because you led me to believe you were bored with that world.'

'Well, I am,' she admitted, 'but—but I don't want to lose it altogether.'

'Of course,' he said, smiling, 'and I will be proud of my wife, be she queen or warrior or songbird or seductress or——' he laughed softly, his hand moving slowly down to touch her silken belly '—or mother to my sons!'

Her eyes closed with rapture at the thought, then fear struck her heart and she asked quickly, 'Suliman—this Sheba. Is her legend the real reason for your love? I mean——'

'How can you even think it?' he said harshly, 'when it was the excuse I used to keep you with me when you would have run?'

'But it's true, isn't it? I mean—I do look like her and—— '

'You look very much like her,' he cut in, 'but it is not the reason I fell in love with you. The power of Sheba is no greater to us than the power of legend in the West. You would not, for instance, sit and dream of St George in England. Yet when you meet your love the image of the knight astride his white horse is powerful indeed.'

'So it really is just me?' she asked huskily. 'Me you love?'

'Bethsheba, I feel love for you. What do I feel for a statue of gold and a legend written on paper so that it crumbles to the touch? No; I used Sheba as the excuse I needed to keep you with me. I could hardly tell you how much I wanted you, how fascinated I had been by you when I saw you in the Press.' He laughed, shaking his head. 'On the cover of *Paris Match*, and I read the article in a café on the *Place d'Étoile*! On the cover of *Life* magazine—and I read the article in the Oak Room of the Plaza, New York.'

'Darling...!'

He smiled down at her. 'I knew I would one day meet you. It was just a question of when.'

Bethsheba almost burst with pride, then said, 'But the part of her legend about her birth...that she was born in a goat-hair tent in Arabia and——'

'It is true,' he said deeply, unsmiling.

There was a little silence.

'Oh...then you didn't make it up?' she asked huskily. 'You didn't get it from my Press clippings and——'

'No, I did not!' he said with cool arrogance. 'If you have read your own Press coverage you will know that Bahrain is the only detail of your birth that is mentioned.'

Destiny vibrated in the air between them and Bethsheba shivered. 'You mean it could be true?'

'That you are the Sheba?' he said softly, touching her. 'It could be. But we will never know, my love. No winged angel will come down with the proof of reincarnation, and no amount of wondering will ever provide you with the answer.' He kissed her deeply, then said under his breath, 'I only know that I love you with all my heart, and that I want you to share my world.'

'Darling, when?' she asked hoarsely. 'When did you know you loved me? Was it before we even met?'

'How could I fall in love with a photograph?' he said, laughing. 'Darling, I am an unusual man, but not that unusual!'

'Then...?'

He studied her, unsmiling. 'I think the moment of real love was when you saved my life by killing the snake in the desert.'

'No!'

'You looked so brave and beautiful in the moonlight with blood on your sword and the courage of a warrior in your eyes!' His hands tightened on her as he said thickly, 'How could I help but feel knocked backwards by a wave of love so great that I could not speak?'

'Darling...' she said shakily, 'that was the moment I knew I loved you too!'

'Then we are truly united!' he said under his breath. 'And it is proof, I hope, that my love defies the legend of Sheba more than it adheres to it.'

'So it's not just my golden hair that attracts you?' she asked huskily.

'My love,' he drawled, 'you are not the only golden-haired woman I have ever known!'

Her eyes darkened with jealousy and she said thickly, 'Oh!'

He laughed, eyes teasing. 'Now you are jealous, my love, and you have no need to be. Not jealous of another woman, not jealous of Sheba. It is you I love, Bethsheba, and only you.'

'No rivals?' she asked, heart thudding.

'Only the desert,' he said softly, 'but it is a love you share, and together we will find everything we need in its golden wilderness.'

'You prefer to live in the desert?'

'Yes, I prefer it,' he said with an amused smile. 'I love the West. I love its art and music and theatre and society. I love the *Champs Élysées* and Harrods and Times Square.' He laughed, drawling, 'Shall I go on? To San Francisco, Hong Kong, Sydney...'

'What's that song about how nice it is to go travelling, but oh, so nice to come home?'

'Exactement!' he said deeply, kissing her. 'For here I am the man I was born to be. Here I am free to ride across the golden wilderness as a man against the elements. No money or power or success can protect me out there. And that is as it should be, for that is as man was born to be.'

She studied him with pride. 'But how deep do the ways of the desert world go, my darling?' She struggled to find the courage she needed to ask the next question as her eyes darkened. 'I—I mean— all those women, are they...?'

'They are not my mistresses,' he said softly, 'though there have been many. But for some reason, my love, I confess, I am a one-woman man. It is not in my nature to take woman after woman. I find it dulls the excitement rather than adding to it. How can a woman truly please me if she feels she is performing for her master rather than sharing a joyful sexual experience?'

Bethsheba flushed, lowering her lashes.

'I like the woman I make love to,' he said deeply, 'to reach fulfilment herself. How can she do that if she is tense?'

She buried her hot face in his throat with a groan. 'And I reached fulfilment with you the first time! Oh, embarrassment!'

He laughed, kissing her. 'My darling, you knew I loved you!'

She raised her head to look at him, eyes on fire with love. 'Can it be true,' she whispered huskily, 'that I have found my love forever?'

'Believe it,' he said fiercely, 'with all your heart! You will stay here in the desert and be my queen, bear me sons! When the West calls we will fly to it! But always we will be together—have no fear of that!'

'You will be my sheikh!' she said huskily.

'And you my warrior queen!'

'Suliman,' she said hoarsely, 'you are everything I could ever have dreamt of in a husband and lover from the moment of my birth!'

'But is that not the way of kismet?' he said thickly, and his hard mouth claimed hers in a kiss that led to other things...

Mills & Boon

Next month's Romances

Each month, you can choose from a world of variety in romance with Mills & Boon. These are the new titles to look out for next month.

SUMMER STORMS Emma Goldrick

PAST PASSION Penny Jordan

FORBIDDEN FRUIT Charlotte Lamb

BAD NEIGHBOURS Jessica Steele

AN UNUSUAL AFFAIR Lindsay Armstrong

WILD STREAK Kay Thorpe

WIFE FOR A NIGHT Angela Devine

WEEKEND WIFE Sue Peters

DEAR MISS JONES Catherine Spencer

CLOAK OF DARKNESS Sara Wood

A MATCH FOR MEREDITH Jenny Arden

WINTER CHALLENGE Rachel Elliot

CASTLE OF DESIRE Sally Heywood

CERTAIN OF NOTHING Rosemary Carter

TO TRUST MY LOVE Sandra Field

STARSIGN

SHADOW ON THE SEA Helena Dawson

Available from Boots, Martins, John Menzies, W.H. Smith, most supermarkets and other paperback stockists.

Also available from Mills and Boon Reader Service, P.O. Box 236, Thornton Road, Croydon, Surrey CR9 3RU.

From the author of Mirrors comes an enchanting romance

Caught in the steamy heat of America's New South, Rebecca Trenton finds herself torn between two brothers – she yearns for one, but a dark secret binds her to the other.

Off the coast of South Carolina lay Pirate's Bank – a small island as intriguing as the legendary family that lived there. As the mystery surrounding the island deepened, so Rebecca was drawn further into the family's dark secret – and only one man's love could save her from the treachery which now threatened her life.

W●RLDWIDE

AVAILABLE IN JANUARY 1992 – PRICE: £3.99

Available from Boots, Martins, John Menzies, W.H. Smith, most supermarkets and other paperback stockists.
Also available from Mills & Boon Reader Service, PO Box 236, Thornton Road, Croydon, Surrey, CR9 3RU

ESPECIALLY FOR YOU ON MOTHER'S DAY

Especially for you on
Mother's Day

OUT OF THE STORM - Catherine George
BATTLE FOR LOVE - Stephanie Howard
GOODBYE DELANEY - Kay Gregory
DEEP WATER - Marjorie Lewty

Four unique love stories beautifully packaged, a
wonderful gift for Mother's Day - or why not treat yourself!

Published: February 1992   Price: £6.40

*Available from Boots, Martins, John Menzies, W.H. Smith,
most supermarkets and other paperback stockists.
Also available from Mills & Boon Reader Service, PO Box 236,
Thornton Road, Croydon, Surrey CR9 3RU.*

4 FREE

Romances
and 2 FREE gifts
just for you!

*You can enjoy all the
heartwarming emotion of true love for FREE!
Discover the heartbreak and the happiness, the emotion
and the tenderness of the modern relationships in
Mills & Boon Romances.*

*We'll send you 4 captivating Romances as a special offer
from Mills & Boon Reader Service, along with the chance to
have 6 Romances delivered to your door each month.*

Claim your FREE books and gifts overleaf...

An irresistible offer from Mills & Boon

Here's a personal invitation from Mills & Boon Reader Service, to become a regular reader of Romances. To welcome you, we'd like you to have 4 books, a CUDDLY TEDDY and a special MYSTERY GIFT absolutely FREE.

Then you could look forward each month to receiving 6 brand new Romances, delivered to your door, postage and packing free! Plus our free newsletter featuring author news, competitions, special offers and much more.

This invitation comes with no strings attached. You may cancel or suspend your subscription at any time, and still keep your free books and gifts.

It's so easy. Send no money now. Simply fill in the coupon below and post it to -
Reader Service, FREEPOST, PO Box 236, Croydon, Surrey CR9 9EL.

NO STAMP REQUIRED

Free Books Coupon

Yes! Please rush me my 4 free Romances and 2 free gifts! Please also reserve me a Reader Service subscription. If I decide to subscribe I can look forward to receiving 6 brand new Romances each month for just £9.60, postage and packing free. If I choose not to subscribe I shall write to you within 10 days - I can keep the books and gifts whatever I decide. I may cancel or suspend my subscription at any time. I am over 18 years of age.

Name Mrs/Miss/Ms/Mr _____ EP18R

Address _____

_____

Postcode _____ Signature _____

Offer expires 31st May 1992. The right is reserved to refuse an application and change the terms of this offer. Readers overseas and in Eire please send for details. Southern Africa write to Book Services International Ltd, P.O. Box 41654, Craighall, Transvaal 2024. You may be mailed with offers from other reputable companies as a result of this application. If you would prefer not to share in this opportunity, please tick box. ☐

mps
MAILING
PREFERENCE
SERVICE